Miracle

by
Alice Lynn

Order this book online at www.trafford.com
or email orders@trafford.com

Most Trafford titles are also available at major online book retailers.

Note for Librarians: A cataloguing record for this book is available from Library
and Archives Canada at www.collectionscanada.ca/amicus/index-e.html

Printed in Victoria, BC, Canada.

ISBN: 978-1-4269-1950-3
ISBN: 978-1-4269-1951-0

Library of Congress Control Number: 2009937630

*Our mission is to efficiently provide the world's finest, most comprehensive book publishing
service, enabling every author to experience success. To find out how to publish your
book, your way, and have it available worldwide, visit us online at www.trafford.com*

Trafford rev. 10/15/09

 www.trafford.com

North America & international
toll-free: 1 888 232 4444 (USA & Canada)
phone: 250 383 6864 ♦ fax: 812 355 4082

This book is dedicated to my family and friends. With their love and support, **anything** is possible.

~

Special thanks to my husband, Don, for lending his hand on my cover idea and being the pillar of support. Thanks to Tom Garro for convincing me to write the story. Thanks also to Cathy Farkas, Steve Schiffhauer, Mary Armstrong, and Jen Garro for their endless patience, moral support and enduring friendship. Thanks guys.

~

"*Animals are reliable, many full of love, true in their affections, predictable in their actions, grateful and loyal. Difficult standards for people to live up to.*"

--- Alfred A Montapert

1

*I*t was a clear, sunny day. Actually a great day to look out over the small bay as it was absent of the slightest hint of fog. The only fog that existed today was that which was inside her head. But, sitting in the cool morning air was allowing her mind to clear a bit. She had a little time to painfully gather herself before she began the day's routine. At least she had made it this far – the first stop of the day. It was an important stop in her daily existence. She sat on the damp, cool cement curb waiting. She tried to put the pieces of last evening together in her mind. How did she allow this to happen again? Ah, yes... it was coming back in pieces inside her aching head as she looked at her worn layers of clothes. The telltale sign of red wine remained in several places. The evening started coming back more quickly to her like a movie in her mind. She remembered that she was just preparing to leave the streets for the evening when she encountered the two men in front of the market. They were leaving the store and she couldn't resist one last opportunity to help maintain her existence. She asked them for some change. Harmless enough. When they turned to her, it was apparent that they had been drinking heavily and were carrying bags that seemed to contain more intoxicants to continue their evening fest. They were casually dressed but appeared to have been well-off by their meticulous grooming. It was easy for her to distinguish a person's status after all these years. One turned to the other and mumbled something about nuisances. However, the other didn't seem to notice. Without much thought he reached into one of the bags and handed her a dark green bottle and laughed the words "Enjoy your evening!" The first man began swearing about giving a thirty dollar bottle of wine to a "vagrant." Her memory tuned in to the word and focused on its meaning. She remembered feeling a slight twinge at the word even at the time, but tightly grasped the offering and made off into the darkness. She knew she should not have taken it but convinced herself that she would sell it for some desperately needed money as she hurried along toward the dimly lit back allies.

"Well," she thought, "that did not work out as planned" as it was clear the temptation contained in the glass was far greater than her other needs at the time. She looked down at her dirty weathered hands and remembered them as they were shaking as she struggled against even smelling what the bottle contained last night. It had been a long time since she left that path – the drugs and alcohol. She surely did not want to relive it, but she just couldn't resist it. It had been so long. It would be ok. She thought she would just have a little bit and would give the rest away – maybe to Mr. B. the next day. He was always so nice. And she talked herself into believing it. It sounded harmless, didn't it?

She didn't remember much after opening the fancy foiled top and removing the cork with an old screwdriver and guzzling down the dark potion inside. Annie shuddered at the thought of falling back into that world and realized it had not changed for her. It had been a year since she had pulled herself out of that hole. Her head was aching and she could still smell the foul liquid coming from her breath. She hoped Mr. B. would not notice her stench or current condition but she was wearing the evidence so prominently on her soiled clothes. However, they were the only ones she had. No options. She tried to forcefully wipe the stains away with her hand. No luck.

She desperately depended upon his kindness and generosity. These were the things that kept her out of the missions that were her only other alternative. She had been there before, lived that alternate life. It was a prison that kept her in contact with that other world with those who always had the *medicine* to make the pain go away. That prison she swore she would never reside in again. However, she always seemed to return there or someplace like it. What could keep her from ever going back to that old life again? She had come so far this time. Something very strong... maybe something very special. Yea, special... like she deserved something *special.* She shook her head. Frowning at the cold cement, she waited and hoped for once he would be late. He was not. She heard a familiar whistle coming toward her and she attempted to compose herself and look up. Hurriedly walking toward her was Mr. Berwitz. He was an older man, somewhat stout and balding. He never seemed to be still and was always huffing as he performed any task. His family had owned the deli here in Porto San Francesco for more than sixty years. He

Alice Lynn

had told her the story of his family business several times
per week over the past year. It was memorized. Family.
Reputation. Honor. Responsibility. The words were like
knives right now in light of her condition. She closed her
eyes tightly and waited dutifully for his daily greeting and
hoping what she knew was coming would just not happen.
Real fear erupted in her stomach and her breathing had
become irregular...

"Good Morning, Annie.... *Annie?*" his voice trailed off
while looking at her stopping short of the gated doorway
taking in the whole of her appearance.

"Good Mornin' Mista B." she weakly replied knowing
she and her present state had been noticed. Without
looking up to meet his gaze, she felt his eyes burning
through her. She sat frozen in discomfort and fear at the
reaction she was sure to come.

His first thoughts were that she had been attacked as
he saw her slumped in front of the store and concern filled
his stomach. Her long, reddish hair was severely more
unruly than usual and even her old worn clothes appeared
to be disheveled beyond their normal state. As he took a
step closer and leaned toward her... the smell snaked up
to meet his nose and he jerked upright to distance himself
from its source. As she looked up at him, a quick visual
inspection of her face and clothes confirmed his suspicions
immediately.

"Annie, I see that I won't need you here today." He said
flatly. He began shaking his head. Although he truly liked
her, there was no way she could be present in the deli today.
The customers always come first and no one could possibly
have an appetite being within five feet of her today. He
began shaking his head as his concern quickly changed

to disapproval. He returned to his routine reaching for the key to unlock the gate that began each day. There was much to do before the deli came to life each day. He entered and quickly shuffled to reach the kitchen to fill the sink basin with warm water. As it filled he paused… it was surely quiet. He had become very accustomed to Annie "*working*" there every day although she wasn't really an employee. She wouldn't agree to work for him officially. He had been reduced to allowing her to perform tasks and in exchange she would take some meat and bread and some small amount of money that equaled pocket change to most people. She called it a trade.

How long had it been? It seemed like a long time. Yes, it had been about ten months his mind calculated. But, it was more than a year ago that he had actually met her. The small coastal city had always had its share of permanent homeless people. They were known to all in the central district. Then, there was always an element of transient people who passed through on their way to some larger urban center due mostly to the subway line that ran directly though the city. Porto San Francesco found itself located between two large metropolitan areas and seemed to be a gateway between the two for these types of people who were seeking or running from something. They became part of the scenery and were not often noticed or acknowledged. They often disappeared as quickly as they appeared either via law enforcement or their own volition. There was not much in this small city to entice them to stay. The big cities seemed to swallow them in with their masses without much notice. This city's permanent occupants seemed to tolerate if not totally ignore their temporary presence.

As he quickly prepared the items for today's offering, he remembered seeing her for the first time in front of the shop. He was sweeping the entryway and sidewalk and locked eyes with her. He immediately recognized she was new and one of the nomadic types that were usually invisible. Yet there was something *different* about her. Over the following weeks, he noticed her each morning and then each afternoon as he was opening and closing the business. Finally one morning he was carrying several boxes while opening the gate when he heard a soft voice behind him.

"Can I help ya with that, sir?" He turned to find her standing there with outstretched hands. Although the customary response would have been "no" or "go away," he was intrigued by the sound of her accent and reassured by the transparency in her eyes.

"Uh... sure." He remembered thinking that he must be crazy, but before he could change his mind she had quickly taken several boxes of napkins and was quickly ushering them in to the counter. She smiled and very quickly excused herself and left. That was the thing. She didn't ask for money or food that day. She just offered him some assistance and left. He remembered it vividly and how unexpected it all was. After that morning, he saw her regularly and exchanged greetings. She would always offer help if he was carrying anything to the store. It was as if she were waiting to be of some assistance to him. As the days went on they began talking more and more. He realized that Annie *was* different in some ways.

Mr. Berwitz without thinking began filling the metal trays behind the counter. His actions were so automatic that it was easy for him to continue this train of thought.

Annie had the initial appearance of vagrancy – her long, wild, reddish hair, thin build, the tattered mismatched layers of clothing, and the accompanying compliment of bags and items she always carried as she scurried along the fringe of daily life in the city. However, upon closer inspection, there was something different about her. He had never really dissected the issue fully but had now become engrossed in it after this morning's events. He artfully began carving a large piece of meat at the slicer and frowned at the effort in identifying exactly what it was about Annie. It was more effort than the physical task he was performing.

His mind's eye scoured over his memories. It was really several things he began to formulate. The first difference, he noted, was that she was not solely a beggar. He had seen her ask for money. Sure. But, it was more of a polite request than actual begging. He had also witnessed that she was willing to perform tasks in exchange for the items she needed to survive. It wasn't a total "hand-out" mentality. Lastly, he had almost subconsciously ignored that she possessed the ability for perfectly acceptable social interaction with only one flaw. She was easily distracted and seemed almost unable to maintain a single train of thought. She jumped from subject to subject without hesitation which took some getting used to but which actually became humorous and enjoyable over time. Her conversational skills were sharp aside from the lack of focus and she possessed a general knowledge that could seem equal to his at times while she was focused on the discussion.

He stopped and stood very still. He had to admit that during these months, he really didn't learn much *about* her. It was more that he got to *know* her. The sight of her at the gate popped back into his mind. Maybe he was wrong to dismiss her so quickly without giving the opportunity for an explanation. Maybe he judged her too harshly. Who knows what she has been through? The scar on her face? How had it happened? It almost had disappeared from his consciousness after all these months. It would never have been proper to ask about it. Really all he knew was that she was from London. That was a question not easily ignored based upon her moderate British accent and its uniqueness in this area. It had come up very early in their acquaintance. Aside from that, he knew nothing more. Maybe it had been safer that way. He was breaking some silent code by befriending her. Maybe if he knew all the answers, he wouldn't have decided to help her.

He glanced at the clock. Five minutes until it would begin. Greetings. Customers. Food. Service. He would think about this more after closing when he didn't need all his attention focused on each person. Service was the cornerstone of his business. He was running behind schedule as Annie had not been there. He coughed out a little laugh realizing that he had come to depend on her more than he realized.

———◆———

Annie had left the deli to return home. She rapidly slunk through the quiet early morning streets until she reached the old warehouse district that had for her become *home*. She realized that the day was doomed and there was no reason to continue on her normal routine and slipped along the side of a small two-story brick office building that had been long abandoned with the warehouses when the manufacturing industry left this area in the 1980's. Or at least that is how the General had described it. In the back of the building among the uncut chest-high weeds, she paused. Her head was pounding and she felt faint from the effort of practically running to her refuge. She started up the few stairs to the entrance and slipped inside. She quietly called out but there was no answer. Surely the General had gone to the pier as was his daily routine. She went quickly upstairs to her "apartment." She pulled the door at the top of the stairs open and entered. There was an instant assault of her senses. The putrid odor of recycled alcohol permeated the air. She began to look around the large one-room area that had become her home just over a year ago. The meager furnishings that the General had helped her reclaim from dumpsters and curbside receptacles were as she left them. However, the dark bottle, the foil and the crumbles of cork remained on the floor near her mattress. A dark red spattered pool on the mattress indicated the outcome of her indulgence and the source of the smell, regardless of her recollection of it. She hurried to crack a window before she became sick again and with the sobriety now to not only remember it but possibly experience it again.

The window would only open a few inches and Annie leaned to gasp at the cool fresh air and the relief it provided. As she regained control of her stomach, she retreated to get a few cushions that she had found months ago and laid them on the floor near the window. She laid on top of them to recover and figure out the best way to clean the mattress before she could consider sleeping on it again. Maybe it would just go away. Yes, maybe it would all just go away. She began to cry and the sobs hurt her head. Surely she deserved it. Punishment. She did it again after she swore it would never happen again. Would she ever learn? Would she ever make it out of this nightmare that had long become her life? The tears burned and she opted to bury her face in the cushions and think about it later. The sobs quieted and the comfort of sleep arrived…

Annie's eyes blinked open at the sound of a thumping noise that resounded inside of her head. She winced and realized that the torture from last night had not completely ended. She lay perfectly still for a moment and realized the thumping was the General. He had probably returned from the pier and as was customary, had begun his formation exercises in his apartment below. Yes, it was he marching to a drill sergeants commands from long ago. It was normally comforting to know he was there and she was not alone. However, today was different. It was proving painful. It was getting dark and she was hungry. She glanced over to the corner of the room and there were five plastic jugs. Four of these jugs were empty and the last containing only several cups of water. She had messed up. There was no food. There was no water as she had not completed the day as she had carefully orchestrated upon her settling in here. A new life… A new beginning… It seemed that now the past had found her here and it was clear that she really could go to hell a second time. Fourteen years of residing there in hell was enough. She decided to just remain there on the cushions and not move. It was safer than venturing out and finding another door to the past. There were so many. She was too weak to resist it again. The streets and the mission were invitations. The desire to find more of the intoxicants that she knew would make her immediate pain go away but would nullify her escape from hell was all too real. She concentrated on the thumping of the General's march to hypnotize her to sleep again and escape until she could regain her senses and some little control over her destiny. She clenched her eyes and begged for a sign. Something to follow. Yes, she was praying. She normally didn't pray, but at this moment, she asked for just a little sign.

She slept for a while. Yet, complete rest would not arrive tonight. She began to dream and thrash upon the cushions. She felt the dreaming state and a desire to wake herself but it was as if someone was restraining her onto the floor. All the random colors and images seemed to fade in on a single image - a hand with a gold, shiny object in it. She sat straight up and gasped looking around to gain her bearings. Yes, she was at home, on her cushions and it was deep into the middle of the night. Annie relaxed and shook her head. It was certainly the continued ill effects of yesterday's wine. She decided to lie quietly until it was time to begin the day. She would go early so she could attempt to make amends with Mr. B. That was first. Then, she would certainly have to find food. Although terribly hungry, Mr. B. came first. She could make it until then or everything she had worked for could be lost and she had no idea if she could ever start over again.

She was up well before daylight. Annie used what water was left to clean up herself and her clothes. Annie frowned that the stain did not come out entirely. She would have to make a trip to the 16th Street Mission to replace them. She hated going there - too many questions. The people who worked there were nice, but always trying to coax her to stay or sign up for some type of assisted living. No way. She had a collection of small bars of soap that still existed in some public restrooms. When she found a source, she quickly took them. She took extra care to prepare herself today. Along one wall of her room, she kept a row of cardboard boxes. Each contained items she had found discarded and that had some use for her. She quickly found a bag of rubber bands and a partial mirror. She swooped her long full hair into the band and checked its placement using the mirror. "Looks ok," she thought. It felt like she was going to an audition. She recalled all those unnerving appointments for auditions when she first arrived in the States. No. She shrugged off the topic before the memories all came back. Those years were gone and she was determined that they stay gone. Focus. She placed one of the plastic jugs inside her large canvas bag and hurried out and down the stairs to get an early start on the day.

She hurried from the weeded path onto the narrow alley that took her to the central district where the streets crisscrossed through the city buildings, businesses and then on to the piers. It was a long walk on foot that required several hours even using short cuts. Annie decided to use the subway. She rarely made use of it. There were only several stops here in the city. The service was mainly for those in transit between the large urban areas to the north and south. It was never full and Mr. B. had told her that they were considering closing it. The long tunnel was costly to upkeep and it did not make enough money to justify its continued use. However, until that time, it was an option for days like today. She hurried along the central district streets where the government buildings were located and the subway had a station. There were only two others... one was near the piers and the other was near a small commuter airport at the eastern outskirts of the city.

Down the stairs and into the tube... There should be an arriving train in about ten minutes. She could wait. It would take her to the pier in fifteen minutes. It was better than walking for more than an hour. She was largely alone. There were several people sitting and waiting but were buried in newspapers and didn't notice her. She checked the trash cans for anything useful. Then she made a quick check of the restrooms for soap or paper towels. No soap today, but she did manage to gain a nice sized stack of paper towels and a brown barrette left on the sink. She pushed them into her bag and returned to wait. She could hear a faint rumbling and knew that her ride was right on time.

She reached her destination and quickly climbed the stairs. She could smell the ocean almost immediately. She quickly went to the pier and found one of the General's friends who were preparing his boat for its daily fishing run. She had time to practice her fence mending skills here before having to face Mr. Berwitz. She had almost forgotten that she did not make it to the pier yesterday to assist the General and Mr. Stillman after the fishing run. It was a daily chore she added to help the General. The fishermen were nice to him and in return for her efforts fed him the remainder of their lunches after their long work day. It was the least she could do after all the General had done for her. Cleaning the bait buckets and mopping decks passed the time until she could return to her sanctuary in the old office building. They also saved her newspapers and magazines and they were coveted entertainment as well as useful after being read. She saved them in a box along the wall in her room.

"Hey, Annie. We missed you yesterday. Even the General didn't seem to know where you had disappeared to" he said smiling as he was wiping down the last section of the smooth boat. The older weathered man hardly missed a beat preparing for the early morning run while speaking. "The catch was small yesterday. So, we were finished early even without your help."

"Yes, sir. I, uh… well, I wanted to say I was sorry for missing yesterday. I… I…" Her voice trailed off and she looked at her hands clenched in front of her trying to find the right words. "I should have been here and I hope that you will let me come back today." Her voice was a little shaky and nervous. What if he said no? The General would be forced to go through the dumpsters again. How could she have messed this up? Her face contorted waiting for an answer.

"Ha ha ha… you must be kidding me right? Hell Annie, you missed one day. I told ya, we had a small catch. It wasn't a problem." He finally turned to look at her and saw the expression on her face. "Hey, don't worry about it. The General picked up the slack and marched several times around the pier while he ate at least five halves of leftover fish sandwiches from the day." Pete Stillman saw immediately that she worried they wouldn't continue their kindness if she did not come to help. "Really Annie," he said, "we've kinda let the old guy grow on us and we like having him here telling the war stories and doing his drills for us. It passes the time. So, yea, you can come back this evening. Maybe we'll have a good catch and there will be plenty for you to do to make up for yesterday! What do ya think about that?"

She exhaled with relief. She wasn't used to people really noticing them. Moreover, these were people really even being *nice* to them. That was why she whole-heartedly loved the pier and the deli. They were the two places that seemed to know they existed and actually helped them exist. No handouts. It was an exchange, participation. It was stability for the first time in years. It was maybe trivial for them but life-sustaining for her. The mission offered handouts that came with a price – loss of independence and the temptations the other residents possessed.

"Thank you, Mr. Stillman. I will be here right on time today – at the top of the hour at six and ready for the biggest catch you ever brought in." She nodded politely. "I have to go now."

"Ok. I think we have roast beef for the crew today. The General is in for a treat!" He smiled and jumped aboard and the boat and its crew began hurrying about the deck readying to get underway on their run.

Annie sighed. A huge relief came over her. However, after two steps she realized that this was just the practice run. There was still Mr. B. He surely would not be so easy. And, she had not done so well at the pier really - mostly lucky that Mr. Stillman was so good-natured. She winced again and hurried along the road back into the Central District to find her place at the deli and begin to repair the damage if possible.

2

Annie rehearsed her lines over and over as she walked the shortcut from the pier to the deli. Her mind raced... "Mr. B., I'd like to tell you sorry for..." That sounded pathetic. Maybe it was best to use his full name. "Mr. Berwitz, I would like to really apologize for not helping you yesterday..." Again, it just seemed to fall short of how she really felt and the true disgust she had for herself and her behavior. Had she arrived already? There was the deli. She was still a little early, but there was hardly time to memorize a speech. Would he believe her? Would he believe that she was truly sorry and allow her back inside to go on with the life she had come to cherish? How could he know it was the one place she felt *normal*. It was a funny word to her – normal. What was that anyway? It had been a long time since she had any kind of *normal* life. Oh God, the sound of footsteps. She took a deep breath. This was it. It had to be okay. It was the most important audition in her whole life.

She immediately stood straight up and turned to meet the source of the sound. It was Mr. Berwitz. She looked at him directly. Given his value for honor and respect, he was not going to accept this apology in any other manner than her taking full responsibility. He stopped short of the gate and they stood quite still looking at each other for what was probably several seconds, but seemed like more like an eternity.

She was beginning to panic more as each second passed and realized that she had to make the first move.

"Mr. Berwitz… Sir… I have come to apologize. I am not sure if I am still welcome here about your place, but what happened yesterday was my fault. I shouldn't have come. Actually, I shouldn't have found myself not able to come here. I guess that is the real problem, isn't it? I am here to tell ya that I will try to make sure that never happens again." The words were racing out of her mouth so fast they were barely intelligible. She felt some confidence that her apology went well. Or did it? He hadn't moved. He wasn't saying anything. The quiet was too much. A second round of rapid thoughts came pouring out…"Uh, Mr. B., I… well, I know this town has its share of people like me and all, but really… I think they are like the snowflakes, don't you? I mean, each one is different. I'm not meaning to bring any nonsense here for ya… I mean…

"Wait." The word was barely audible, but it stopped Annie cold. Mr. Berwitz looked at her for a moment. "Annie, there are some things we need to talk about. I have thought it over. Before we can make any progress here, we definitely have to talk. After we do that, I will decide what I think is best. I have to prepare for the day and open the store. You can come back here tonight at eight. The deli will be closed but I'll be here finishing up."

The words were like stones hitting her face. She tried to hide her face a little but her hair was securely bundled and there was really no curtain to hide behind at the moment.

"Yes sir. I will be here at eight," as she looked quickly down at the sidewalk feeling like a child waiting for a good scolding. She bit her lip to keep her mouth from starting the explanation and apology again.

"Alright then – eight o'clock. We will get this over with." He turned quickly toward the deli and his feet quickly began for the entrance. It seemed less than an instant and he had gone inside.

This had not gone well. Not at all. Annie stood frozen in front of the deli. Had she ruined everything in one careless night? Had she lost all hope for building a normal life here in Porto San Francesco? Where was there left to run? Where could she go to start over? She felt exhausted and knew that she didn't have the strength to start over again. She didn't have the strength to move. She hadn't eaten for well over a day and there was no water left after she had cleaned up for this most important morning. She clenched hers eyes tight when the mental picture of the mission appeared in her head as the only answer. Food, water, and clean clothes. And, all of the temptations that seemed to keep her from all that she wanted just outside the mission's front door. There was no where left to go.

Annie hadn't moved an inch. Her head began pounding and the knot in her stomach turned quickly to a sick feeling that spread outward. It started slowly and then turned into wave that flooded over her. The humming in her ears was deafening and the tingling in her hands and feet were like electric. She opened her mouth to call out but it all stopped instantly.

"Annie? Annie? Can you hear me?" The voice seemed so far away. Annie tried to zero in on it but it just kept getting fading in and out.

"Jacob, from what I can see here outside of the hospital without any testing is that she is really quite dehydrated and possibly suffering from low blood sugar. My examination is rudimentary you understand. However, after removing the layers of clothing, she is really very thin. There is a possibility of malnutrition as well. I left her sleeping. Rest is probably good for now, but she is going to need to get some fluids and something light into her system soon."

"It was so fortunate that you found her. I mean, I just left her outside several minutes before you came. She seemed fine. I told her to come back early this evening. I mean, I am still in shock, Mendel. Is she going to be okay?"

"Listen, I see this kind of patient fairly often at the hospital. They don't take the best care of themselves, you know? They live a pretty tough life out there and over the years, the body just wears out." Dr. Mendel Kauffman was looking directly at his friend, Jacob Berwitz. It was hard not to see the sympathy or maybe guilt that seemed to cover his face. "Look, Jacob, I could check out the hospital resources and see if there is some type of social program that could offer her some assistance. I mean, are you really going to keep this woman here in the apartment above the deli?"

This was a good question. It was one that the deli owner had not considered until this moment. It had all happened so suddenly. He heard Dr. Kauffmann call out and when he reached the doorway saw Annie lying on the sidewalk. It was autopilot from that point forward. He leaned down and swept her up and with the doctor's help took her up to the upstairs apartment that had been vacant for several months. It was furnished and made for a private area for the doctor to assess Annie's condition.

"You know... I don't know. I mean, I don't know what to do." He remembered some vague references that Annie had made over the past months about her dislike of the mission and her love of freedom. But, what was *best* for Annie may well be different than what she *wanted*.

"Who is she, Jacob?"

This was the question that had been plaguing Jacob Berwitz for the past 24 hours. "Annie. Her name is Annie. She, well... she just kind of showed up here like a stray cat. I mean, I don't get involved with *them*, you know? But she was different. So, she's been helping out here every day. It was fine until yesterday. She showed up and was a mess. The smell of alcohol almost knocked me off my feet and she looked like she had slept in a dumpster. I mean, what would you have done? I sent her off. I can't have someone like that at the deli. I told her we would discuss this later this evening. Then, this happened."

"Hmmm... well, I hope you know what you are getting yourself into. No offense Jacob. It is just a risk. I appreciate that you wanted to help her out. But, hell, you don't even know her last name, do you?"

"She might have mentioned it. I don't know. She just talks in circles all morning while she does some chores here before the deli opens. She sometimes runs errands during the day. But, that was why I asked her to come this evening. I had questions that needed answers. I never expected this."

"This could be a headache, Jacob. Do you want me to make a call to the hospital?"

Jacob Berwitz paused and thought hard. He needed to decide. Although the easiest thing to do would have been to allow Dr. Kauffmann to "fix" this, it wasn't an easy decision.

"Well, I would think it best that I wait until she comes around and ask her what she wants to do. I can tell you Mendel that she is somehow *different* than many of those you see at the hospital. She has been here for months and nothing like this has happened. I think I will wait until this evening and talk with her. If I think that she is going to be a problem, I'll call you tomorrow morning and we'll make that call. Okay?"

"Sure. Whatever you think is best. I can respect your willingness to help her out. Just think it all the way through. Well, I am going to be late. I have the early shift at the hospital today. I was actually coming for a quick bagged breakfast and then head in for my shift. Oh, I see I am definitely late. I have to go now."

"Let me get you something for your trouble. It won't take two seconds. I appreciate your help with this." The deli owner was already hastily downing the stairs and making a mental list of the items he could pack up quickly in hopes of repaying Dr. Kauffmann's kindness and diplomacy.

The moment the doctor was out of the door, Jacob Berwitz knew exactly what he had to do next. He directed the two deli workers in haste as he marched to the telephone in the back.

"Emily. I need you at the deli right away. No, I'm fine. Yes, the deli is fine. I just need you here as quickly as you can get here. Oh… and bring those two bags of old clothes we were going to drop off at the mission. Yes, of course. You can drive the car and park in the central lot. Yes, I will meet you there in 20 minutes. Yes, I'll explain when you get here." He replaced the handset and went up to check on Annie. Sleeping. Dr. Kauffmann was right about one thing. This was more than finding a stray kitten. He knew he was in over his head on this one. This was definitely something more appropriate for Emily. He knew his wife could help him out of this predicament. He tapped his foot while waiting in the lot but sighed a little relief upon seeing their car slowly creep into the lot.

"Jacob, what has happened?" Her face was tight and he knew he had probably frightened her. "Em, something, well, odd. I just need your help. Remember the woman who cleans up for me at the deli?"

"Yes, that poor soul… um… Amy, no, Annie? Right?"

"Yes, well, it appears that she has become ill. Nothing catchy. Just worn out. She must have fainted or something. Well, good thing Mendel had stopped by and found her right away. I mean, before the deli had opened and we took her up to the apartment upstairs. Look, she is a woman and I just don't feel right… Well you know. She is a little dirty and needs some clothes and a good bath then probably something to eat…" He was uncomfortable thinking of the steps that needed to come next and he stopped just short of the apartment entrance next to the deli still clenching the bags he had taken from the car. "I know it seems odd, but I just can't stand by and do nothing. She is..."

"Poor thing. Is she up there *alone?*" Emily Berwitz pushed ahead of her husband and began climbing the stairs. She was already making a list of what needed to be done aloud as she purposefully rounded the first flight of stairs and began the second. Jacob knew he had definitely called the right person for the job. There wasn't a stray cat she couldn't rescue including him at this moment.

Once inside the room with the door shut and her bags settled, Emily sat at the edge of the bed and waited for Jacob to bring the list of items she requested - soup, soda, crackers and soap. She waited quietly until she saw the woman stirring in the bed.

"Annie, Annie." The woman opened her eyes and took almost a minute to focus in to meet hers.

"Oh, where am I? Oh, excuse me ma'am. I... I... don't know..."

"Annie. I am Emily Berwitz. I am Mr. Berwitz's wife. He called me here because you seemed to be ill this morning. Don't worry dear. You are in the apartment above the deli. You are completely safe. How do you feel?"

Annie tried to sit up, but quickly felt dizzy and fell back onto the pillows.

"Oh please, dear, just relax a moment. I have some soup here and I think it will fix you right up. How about a little bit to see how it goes?"

"Uh, I hate to be a bother ma'am. I ..."

"Well you are not a bother and we are going to try a little soup." Emily sat poised with the spoon in hand.

Annie dutifully nodded and followed the polite orders of her hostess.

———❖———

As Mr. Berwitz was reorganizing after the lunchtime rush, he heard footsteps coming down the apartment stairs. He quickly went to the door and peered up the darkened hallway. Coming down slowly hand in hand were Emily and Annie. He waited to assess the situation since he had been removed from it to keep the business flowing. They reached the doorway.

"Annie. How are you feeling?" Mr. Berwitz asked her with genuine concern. He seemed to look her over briefly from head to toe.

"Actually Mr. B., I am feeling much better. I am so sorry... well, for this and for yesterday and everything, ya know?"

He noticed she had some color and amazingly enough, the clean clothes were an improvement. They weren't an exact fit, but definitely an improvement in appearance and aroma. Even her hair seemed much more tame than normal. Mrs. Berwitz had worked some magic. Annie looked *almost* normal. "Look, Annie... I may have overreacted. And, as far as the explanations... They can all wait. I think we get things back to normal soon and iron this out..."

"There is nothing left to explain. She will be here in the morning as usual." Emily Berwitz matter-of-factly stated. "She has told me everything and there is no reason for her to go through that again, Jacob." Emily patted Annie's hand. "It'll be alright, dear. Now, before you are on your way, let us get you something for later to eat. You'll need something since you only had soup." Mrs. Berwitz proceeded into the deli and went behind the counter carefully selecting a meal for her patient.

Annie and Mr. Berwitz stood dutifully at the door and Emily Berwitz returned with a large bag. "Now, here's something for later. Don't worry about the General. I put some extra things in there for him as well if you can't make it to the pier. And, I will send you some things from time to time with Jacob to the deli – clothes, coats, toiletries. So, make the most of this second chance, Annie. You can do it."

Annie reached out numbly to take the large bag from Mrs. Berwitz. She hadn't said a word, but her mind was going in a hundred directions. She managed to get out a soft "thank you." All she could see was the look on Mr. B's face - full of confusion, just blankly looking at his wife. She would tell him. That was sure and so much easier. It had been a long two days. She was exhausted. There was time to go back to the office building and put the day together and rest before she had to be at the pier. Even though she promised Mrs. Berwitz she would not go today. It was almost like having parents again. And she quietly turned and started for home. She tried to remember them... the images were cloudy. Maybe later.

It was six o'clock and she was standing on the pier. The breeze was cool but with the new clothes, she was not cold. It felt nice. In the distance she could see the boats coming in to dock with their day's catch. And, right on time, she turned to see the General walking the planked path to the pier.

"Annie. I have been looking for you for days! I told them that you were probably captured and behind enemy lines. Are you hurt? Did you escape?"

"Yes, they did have me for a while, General. But, I did what you told me. Name, rank and serial number. I think they got tired of me and when they weren't looking, I ran off!"

"You are a good girl, Annie. You would have made a fine sailor."

"Thank you, General."

"Well, then. It is good to have you back. Now I just have to whip these guys into shape. Their tactics are sloppy. They act like there is no danger. It is all about discipline, you know."

"Yes, sir." Annie smiled and the image of Mr. Stillman became clear on the deck. He was waving to the General who began barking out orders as if he were on the deck with them. It was time to get to work.

It had been an endless day. Annie was exhausted after her work at the pier. She wasn't as helpful as usual, but no one seemed to notice. She could now go home. The walk seemed almost painful. She wondered if she had missed the last train. She mustered enough energy and rushed to the subway entrance in the hopes to rest while the machine took her home. Down the stairs and inside. It was late and the station was empty except for a few stragglers. She sat on the step and waited to see if she had made it for the last ride of the night – 10 p.m. She needed a watch. Her thoughts jumped from moment to moment repeating her day in some random order. She closed her eyes.

She heard some kind of sound coming from beyond the platform. At first she thought she had imagined it. But, there it was again. It sounded like someone gargling, no maybe growling. It was getting a little louder. She was tired, but there was some curiosity that kept her focused on the sound. She didn't wander the tunnel. It wasn't safe. There were people much worse down here than on the streets. The street thugs were obvious. They were easy to identify and to avoid. This space was confined and there was often nowhere to run. It was more dangerous. There was no help in the cold stone floor and walls. There were no witnesses.

Although she knew better, she kept hearing the noise off and on and her curiosity won over her fear and exhaustion. What *was* that? She got up and walked past the platform to the narrow walk that lined the tracks. It was getting darker and she felt a little afraid. But, her curiosity kept her feet moving forward slowly. There it was again. It was no more intelligible than before – a gargle or a growl? She slowly crept forward waiting for the sound to direct her.

She was squinting into the almost darkness when the noise erupted almost next to her causing her to jump away. She blinked several times and looked at what appeared to be a boy lying on the cement about five feet in front of her. She inched closer. She could see the ball of his figure in the dim light.

"Hello?" She almost whispered. "Are you okay?" Again, barely audible. The boy lay motionless for several minutes.

Then she heard the noise again. It was some type of sound that didn't seem possible from a human body. In any case, it did not sound *good*.

"Hello? You there? Are ya all right?" She got very close to the tightly clamped body and knelt down beside it. "Hey there. Can ya hear me?"

A soft moaning sound emitted from the lump on the floor. Then, the sound of the approaching train off in the distance. "Hey, I got to go now boy. Are ya alright?" Again, a soft moaning sound that was much more human. The train was getting closer. She was going to have to make a decision. Leave the boy and get to the platform to collect her bags and catch the last car of the night or to stay here and see what was going on with this motionless body on the floor in front of her. The train rumbled closer.

"Well, be damned." She muttered and turned to walk back to the platform. But, something had caught her attention. There was something that had caught the little bit of light remaining in the tunnel and she turned to see what it was. It was barely visible, but there was something shiny. She turned back around and knelt down. The dark ball had not moved. But as she looked at him and reached part way out. She saw something clenched in his hand. Something gold and shiny. She reached her hand to touch it and was startled that the hand responded by opening. In it was a gold shiny object. It was hardly identifiable in this light. It was rounded, no, oval, gold and shiny… yes. She thought she knew what it was. Even here in the almost darkness. A religious medal of some kind in the open hand of this stranger. This was too weird and she started to turn and walk toward the platform. Last chance to get home if she hurried. She grabbed her bags and waited for the nearing train. The doors opened and she hopped on. The jostling of the car was almost like a cradle and she almost instantly fell asleep in the seat. The colors and sounds began and then the whole dream focused on a shiny golden object held in someone's hand. She jerked up in the seat and gathered herself. Where was she? Thankfully she noted the familiar advertisements and realized it had only been minutes since she had fallen asleep. She got off at the next Central stop and hurried back to the original pier entrance to see if she was not too late to find him again.

3

*A*nnie quickly ran down the stairs. She looked around and saw that no one remained after the last car had left. The only people that would be here now were the ones she would do well to avoid. But, for now, the coast was clear. She hurried to the platform and looked down into the tunnel entrance and listened for any sound. Nothing but eerie quiet. Oh no. Was he still there? She tip-toed along the wall into the darkened tunnel. She strained to adjust her eyes to the darkness. She didn't see anything. She didn't hear anything. She moved slowly forward ignoring her fear but feeling a sense of panic that she would not find this person who may have been the key to everything. Why did she leave? She began muttering to herself that she had really made the worst mistake in her life... and then there was a soft sound ahead.

Annie carefully felt her way along the wall. It was completely dark now. She moved slowly until her foot hit something. Something kind of soft. She knelt down and reached out to feel what her eyes could not see. Yes, it was a body. It had to be him.

"Hey, I see you may need some help. I'm Annie. Are ya ok? Can you talk?" There was a small whisper that she couldn't really understand that came as a reply.

"Ok then. I guess the first thing to do is to get you out of here and then we can go from there. Can you walk?" Again, a soft sound was her answer.

"Ok, I guess I am going to have to help you up or something here. I am not trying to hurt ya or anything." She began to feel him along his body to find his arms and chest to see if she could lift him up. She noticed that he was no longer tightly balled up and that he felt bigger than she had thought before. She reached around his chest and was surprised that he was so slim and light. She was able to get him upright.

Ok, now what? She fought in her mind to figure out what to do now that she had semi-pinned him against the wall. Could she lift him? Could she carry him? She turned her back to him to see if she could put him on her back and realized that he was actually too big for that. Not too heavy, just too tall. She knew she wouldn't be able to carry him alone. She sat him back onto the narrow walk along the wall. She had to think.

She needed help. Surely she and the General could get him back to the office building. But she would have to leave him here and make the long journey on foot and then back again. Would he still be here? It was a risk. She could wait there with him, but in the daylight hours, there would be many more people in the station and it would attract some very negative attention. That would not work.

She had to take the risk of leaving him until she could return with the General.

"Ok, now this is it. You are going to have to trust me, ok? I have to leave to get help. It is going to take me a while to get back. But, I *will* come back with help. I need you to do one thing… if you even understand me. I need you to listen. You can't go moving further into the tunnel. It will be too hard to find ya again and dangerous for all of us. One fall in here could put us right on the tracks. Ok? So I need ya to stay put. Right here, just until I can get back. Another thing. Be quiet in here. There are people that comes in the middle of the night that will not be nice to you. They can't see you right now. So, those are the two things I am askin' ya. Be still and be quiet until I can get back for ya, ok?"

She scurried from the station. She alternated between walking and running as much as she could. She was exhausted from her day at the deli, but her focus was upon the image of his hand that held the object she saw in her dream. This was her chance for something that was being sent to her. She refused to be distracted so she could stay focused on getting to the General.

Annie was gasping but managed to climb the stairs and fling the door to the office building open. Out of respect, she rarely entered far into the first floor area. It was the General's place. But, she was short on time and manners at the moment. She wondered how long it had taken her to get here. She stopped and thought about needing a watch. She shook her head almost violently and started past the stairs to her room.

"General? General? GENERAL!!!" Annie screeched his name so loud the last time that her throat hurt. She heard a loud set of thumping noises to her right and followed the sound in the dark building.

A door flew open and a voice barked out. "Who is it?"

"General, it is Annie. General, sir, there has been a terrible thing. I need your help. Oh please General, could you go to the subway station with me? I know it's late and all, but General please help me." Annie bent over forcefully to catch her breath.

"Annie. What has happened? Is it the enemy? Are they advancing? Did they capture you again?"

"No, sir. But they did get someone else. I managed to hide him. I think they hurt him real bad. I need your help to rescue him or surely they will come back for him." She hated to use this method of gaining his help, but she was desperate.

"We leave no man behind, Annie. Is he wounded? Do we need to get him to a medic?"

"General, I think he is hurt, but I was wanting to bring him back here. I don't think it's safe anywhere else. If that is okay with you, I mean. I know this is your place. You were so kind to help me when you found me. I know it's a lot to ask." Annie had not considered this part. The General did not allow any visitors. This place was his headquarters. No one could know about it. It would 'compromise their safety' as he had lectured her many times. Would he say no? Her mind started going in a thousand directions again wondering what else could she do? She almost didn't hear him speak and had to stop herself.

"What did you say?"

"Annie, I asked if the man was down?"

"I don't know what you mean. I mean, yes. He can't seem to walk or talk. But, he's alive and needs help. General, I really must get back there. Please, will you help me?"

The General was very still. She couldn't really see his face in the dark room to get any idea what he was thinking. She was barely able to keep herself from screaming waiting for some kind of answer. She was still panting from the effort to make it here.

"Well, if you are *sure* it was the enemy and he is not some kind of trick or spy. Annie, you know they are cunning, the enemy. Are you sure he is one of *ours*?"

"Yes. Yes I am. But, you can see for yourself, General. Please come with me and see for yourself."

"Hmmm… Alright. I will go with you to see. We do not leave a man behind. I will come with you and assess the situation. He could be a plant. They can be difficult to spot. *If* he is one of ours… we will bring him back here to await further orders. Let me get my gear…"

Annie released a sigh of relief. She hoped her luck would not run out before she could get back to the station and *then* hope the General saw him as she did – as one of them.

Annie and the General descended the stairs to the station. They were both winded from the pace to get here. However, they had both slowed to barely a crawl going down the stairs. They were both well aware of the potential for danger in these places in the middle of the night. The

General had donned his camouflage jacket and had a good grasp upon an ancient baton. He told Annie many stories about using that item in hand-to-hand combat in the jungle. She actually felt afraid and a little sorry that she had to bring him here. What if they did run into some trouble? She was a small woman and he was an old man. They were really breaking all the rules of self preservation. She almost wanted to tell him to stop. They could run away and go home. Unharmed. But, something deep inside kept telling her that she *had* to risk this. Her face seemed to ache from the pained expression upon it.

"Ok Annie. Where is he? Where did you hide him?"

"He's over here. I left him down a ways in the tunnel. It was dark and I hoped no one could see him there."

"That's dangerous, Annie."

"Yes, sir. I know. I didn't know what else to do."

"Ok, show me."

Annie walked across the platform and toward the tunnel. The General followed a few yards behind her. She walked more slowly now that the light from the platform was not able to penetrate the dark tube under the city. How far along did she leave him? She walked slowly so not to kick him if he were closer than she remembered. Her hand found the wall and she again started to take small, soft steps. Was he still here? She couldn't call out for fear of angering the General with sloppy tactics. Her teeth hurt from the pressure from her jaw.

Thud. Her foot hit the familiar target from earlier this evening. She whispered.

"Here he is. General. Here he is!"

"Shhhh. Annie. Keep it low." The General knelt down beside her on the narrow pathway along the tracks.

"Son? Can you hear me?" A soft moan answered the General's inquiry.

"Son, are you hurt?" The General began to move next to him. Annie couldn't see what he was doing but heard the rustling noise of some kind of movement.

"He's not armed. I don't feel any weapons or listening devices. He is so skinny. It seems they have had this boy for a long time. Probably was in captivity and tortured for a long time. Anyone who could have survived this needs our help and is surely one of ours. Let's get him back to HQ."

Annie felt like she had just won the lottery. She was exuberant. She didn't feel tired or sick right now. She was ready for the impossible task of getting him home and ready for the mystery that lie ahead willed to her by some kind of fate. Maybe Mrs. Berwitz was right. She would get her second chance at doing something right.

———

It seemed like an eternity getting him to safety. They took the darkest streets so not to be noticed with the General taking his shoulders and Annie taking his legs. They must have stopped and started a million times before they had arrived at their destination.

"Alright Annie. We managed to get him here before daylight. Let's take him to the far room on the left."

Somehow Annie felt a strange sense of objection. "But... General... I thought we could get him upstairs to my room where I could take care of him, ya know?"

"Nonsense! I won't be putting men in women's quarters. It isn't right." He barked it out so quickly she jumped when he answered.

"Yes General, you are right. I can make up a room where ever you want to put him. I just assumed that I would be on your nursing staff. I didn't mean to break any of the rules. Sorry."

The General opened the door and picked up his end and moved him into a room in his living space. Annie had never been in this room before. The sun was just beginning to come up and she could see a little of the room and its furnishings. There was a cot along the wall and the General nodded toward it. They placed him on the cot and Annie was getting her first real look at him. She squinted and then looked at the General.

"Ok, Annie. Now, this is the infirmary. He will stay here. You can come to this room and care for the soldier. I will bring you supplies for today. I expect daily updates on his progress and will file my report with the high brass. You will let me know of anything suspicious right away, right?"

"Oh, yes sir. I will."

The General disappeared and then reappeared with several jugs of water and then several bags. He handed them to Annie and nodded and left the room.

There was a little more light and Annie sat on the edge of the cot. She began to realize that this was not a *boy*. This was... a *man*. He was just very thin and had folded himself so tightly in the tunnel that she mistook him for a boy. Ok. Now what? Annie was no nurse. But, she did have some street smarts and decided to use that to the best of her ability. She could work this out, right?

"Hello again. I am Annie. I told you I would get you out of there. Thank you for not moving and being quiet. I guess I need to *check* you. I mean, well to see if you are okay. I am not going to hurt you. If you can, can you answer me?"

A soft unintelligible whisper came from the man. His eyes were shut. It seemed like a cue to continue. Annie began to remove his jacket. He was completely limp like a rag. She checked the pockets for some clue as to who he was. Nothing. She removed the rest of his outer wear and again his pockets were empty. She remembered seeing his hand and upon checking them, found the familiar oval object still clutched in his right hand - a medal of St. Christopher and a plea for protection written upon it. There was an indentation in his hand from where he had forced it so tightly to remain. Who knows how long he had held it there. She grabbed the water and brought it over to the cot. She found soap, a razor, a rag, some crackers, a straw and what appeared to be a bed pan in the bags. She hadn't considered the bed pan. She let that image leave her and began cleaning up the patient in the General's infirmary. He would check on her nursing skills at his first opportunity. The man lay motionless and silent. She began to hum to him as she became consumed in her work. She remembered Mrs. Berwitz and her bedside manner not one whole day ago. She tried to mimic what she remembered from her own recent past. There was so much to do and so little time. The sun was rising and she *must* make it to the deli. No mistakes today. She was exhausted and hungry. Where was her ... Oh, yea. She had left the evening's food in the subway car when she made her hasty exit. Well, her patient was cared for and she was quickly making her way to the deli. She could not afford to lose her focus today. Annie stopped for a brief moment. She was tired. She gathered herself and decided that she could do this. Yes, she would do this for *him*. She would make it through this morning at the deli. She would get them something to eat. She would rest and make it to the pier. Then she could return in the evening to spend her time getting to know him and why he was here. Something about that thought made the day seem less heavy. She was at the deli door. She perched herself on the walk and waited for Mr. B. The sound of familiar footsteps was in the distance. She could really do this…

Annie's day was long. It was moreover the anticipation of returning to the focus of all her thoughts than the exhaustion that reached her bones. She felt distracted but managed to stay focused at the deli and to convince Mr. B. that she was very well and had rested completely after leaving the deli. She had decided not to mention the evening's events. What would Mr. B think? He was so proper. No maybe just *normal*. How could he understand what *normal* was in her world? Not a chance. Not a word about it. She raced with what little energy she had left after she had finished at the deli with her much needed bag of sandwiches. It was good Mr. B. thought she needed to eat more and gave her two extra sandwiches. She could try to get him to eat and hopefully be the good nurse the General expected and that she wanted to be for this stranger.

She sat next to the cot and gobbled down the first sandwich. He had not changed since she had left him this morning. He was very still and almost lifeless. She grabbed a sandwich and sat on the cot. "Um… hey. I'm back here with ya. I know you need to eat. I think you have managed to be even thinner than me. I am going to try to feed ya a little somethin'. Prop you up and all. Here…" She ripped the large, breaded block into small pieces and put them in his mouth. He didn't do anything at first so she rubbed his cheek a little and he began to chew. She got one of the freshly filled water jugs and a straw left by the General and he drank much more than he ate then back to sleep. She looked at him for a while and fell asleep quietly next to the cot on the floor. She awoke and quickly checked him. The same. She was up and out of the building.

The General was perched in his usual spot on the pier and the boats were just in sight. He asked about the soldier and she gave him the update on his condition. He seemed concerned but pleased that she had made progress with him. The evening seemed to drag on and she just wanted to go back and see him again.

She was finally there and seemed to be developing a plan for a routine. She cleaned him up and repeated the earlier method she used to get him to eat. She left him and quietly went to her room to sleep. She wondered what was going to happen. Could she really do this? Was he going to be okay? And then she gave in to the exhaustion.

The following months flew by. Annie sat on the floor near the cot in the early morning light watching him… studying him. It had become part of her daily routine. She was learning his responses during these times. He had begun to open his eyes and look at her when she spoke to him or touched him. She also learned that the condition she found him in inside the tunnel was not fear. It had happened on several occasions since she had brought him to the office building. The first time scared her beyond belief. The trashing and growling noises were terrifying.

And, at their worst, his body would seem to compress itself into an unbelievably small ball and he would barely move. The only sign of life would be the continued sounds that seemed beyond human origin. She did not report these "incidents" to the General. Surely he would want to take him away. But, because Annie knew what they did with people like them she was afraid. He would be tucked away in some State home and never be seen again. She wouldn't let that happen. She found him. He *belonged* to her now. Annie sat quietly studying his face. He had changed in the months he had been with her. He was less pale and sunken than that first night. She also began to notice that when he opened his eyes to look at her, he was actually a little handsome. His brown eyes sometimes focused upon hers and there was something deep in them. His long hair almost covered them at times. She was grateful for this during the fits he seemed to have. His eyes would roll backward and they seemed unfocused and absent. As much as it was frightening to her, it was also sad. She liked when he looked at her and seemed to listen to her while she talked. She also liked holding his hand which would sometimes respond and return the grasp.

He. He? Annie considered that all this time, she thought of him as only *he*. It had just occurred to her that she did not know his name.

"That's it. Today is the day I will figure out a name for ya. I want it to be a good name. So, I'm going to think about it all day while I am out and let ya know when I get back. Ok?"

His eyes opened to look at her and it was one of those moments that Annie had come to love. This was the reason she worked to keep her schedule and her distance from anything and anyone who could send her back into the old life and lose this. She had a purpose for the first time in her life that had nothing to do with herself. And, for the first time, he reached his shaky hand over toward hers. She was surprised at first. He hadn't moved much on his own since she brought him there. Well, except for the fits. She quickly took his hand and they stayed silently looking at each other in the dimly lit room.

"Good morning, Annie."

Annie quickly stood up and waited while Mr. Berwitz reached the deli gate.

"Morning Mr. B." Annie smiled at him and was anxious to get to her tasks so she could begin thinking about what to name him. Maybe something Mr. B. would say could help her think of something. Or maybe just one of the customers. It was nice now that she had been allowed to stay after opening time and work while the deli was open. It seemed...*normal*, she thought. She smiled again.

"You know something, Annie?"

"Yes sir, Mr. B?"

"I have to admit that I thought you wouldn't make it. You know. From what happened before. But, I have to say that I am amazed at how you have changed since that day. I see you are making good use of the things Mrs. Berwitz has been sending you." Mr. Berwitz noticed that Annie had been carefully dressing herself in the hand-me-downs from his wife. It was a definite improvement from the dirty layered look he had endured in the beginning. She even acted differently these past months. She was more focused although she still could make his head swim when she had a periodic loose moment. He smiled back at her as they stood at the gate. He was anxious to get inside and give her the item Mrs. Berwitz had selected that he now held in his pocket.

"Ok Annie, shall we?" He reached up and unlocked the gate and began opening the door. He would give the gift to her inside, privately.

"Sure Mr. B. It is a lovely day. And, yes sir. I see things a bit differently these days. This is my second chance ya know. I am gonna make the most of it. Thanks to you and the missus. I won't let ya down. I think there will be rain today…"

He laughed and stopped her short before she began wiping the chairs and tables.

"Annie, I have something for you. Well, something from me and Mrs. Berwitz."

Annie walked over to him curiously.

"Mr. B. You have given me quite enough already. You don't have to do nothing like this…"

"Nonsense. Annie, it is not a million dollars or anything. Just something from us to show our appreciation. You don't let me pay you much and it seems… well, it is just something I wanted to do."

He held out his hand.

Annie looked into the hand and saw something golden and shiny in it. She moved closer to look at it. She stopped dead and looked up at him with a pained expression.

"Annie. It is not expensive. So, don't look like that. Just take it."

He reached his hand out toward her further. She slowly lifted her hand to receive what he was holding. It was a watch. A beautiful watch. As it left his hand and she felt its cool weight in her hand, she could only stare at it.

"Ok, let me help you get it on. I don't want you to worry anymore about being late." He took the watch from her hand and stretched it over her hand and onto her wrist. It was a little loose. But, it was the smallest watch they saw at the local department store.

"Well? What do you think?

She couldn't' talk. She just looked at it blankly.

"Annie, don't you like it? I mean, I know… we knew that you have always said you needed one." He wondered if it were a mistake to give it to her and began to frown. Maybe they didn't think this one through. He was confused now and felt uncomfortable.

"Mr. B…" She stopped and looked up.

"Mr. B." She began again. "This is the most beautiful gift I have ever got." She thought for a moment and then decided it was the second most beautiful gift she had ever received.

"I just don't know what to say. It is too much, Mr. B. You really shouldn't have done it. I mean… I don't… deserve something like this."

Mr. Berwitz eased hearing her say she liked it.

"Nonsense. I just expect you to keep coming on time. Oh, and Mrs. Berwitz has sent another bag of clothes. It has the men's clothes as well. Does your friend… The General. Yes, does he find them useful?"

Annie flinched and didn't look at him.

"Uh, yes… The General makes good use of 'em. Thank you." She had to look away so he didn't see the lie. She had told them about the General so she could have an excuse to get the men's clothes. She was not going to tell them about *him*. She decided to change the subject before he could read her face.

"Well, I am gonna have to earn this gift. So, I am off to cleaning the tables. Thank you Mr. B."

"You are welcome, Annie." He smiled again at her and went behind the counter to prepare the daily stock.

Annie quickly began to wipe all the tables and chairs. She knew each item from top to bottom. So, she was quickly able to remember her task of the day while her hands kept moving automatically. What should she call him? She let her mind wander and it ended up in the usual place. Remembering things long ago. Before all of this. Her home. Her family. How different life was then. She struggled to remember the images she usually kept locked away. It was so long ago. She thought about her school. The long years there that seemed to be the foundation for the higher education at Sussex. It didn't turn out that way. She decided not to think about that choice. It was almost 20 years ago. She just wanted to think about the time before she had come here. These were her pleasant memories. Odd. They were something to run from then and something to run to now. Surely there could be something there that might help her find a name for him. Nothing. She kept working and hoping that something would come to her.

Customers came in and went out. She was on the second stage of her chores. Mopping the storage area and kitchen were also mindless. She continued thinking back. School was one of her favorite memories. She had loved it. Well, not all of it. Actually it had always been the arts that had mesmerized her. Literature, theater, music, and painting – those were the things she had loved back then. She was able to go through them one by one, remembering small bits and pieces.

"Annie?"

She stopped and looked up. She saw Mr. Berwitz and Dr. Kauffmann standing at the doorway.

"Yes?"

"Ha ha ha. The doctor had asked you a question. You were so interested in that floor that I don't think you even heard him. Ha ha ha."

"I'm so sorry, I… well, just was lost in my head. If you'd please, ask me again."

"Annie, I was just asking Jacob how you were coming along. He said you have been doing well these past months. I just wanted to say hello. I see that he wasn't kidding when he said you had made the most of your second chance" Dr. Kauffmann had come to pick up something for his shift at the hospital as he did when he worked the day shift.

"Yes, doctor. And, thank you again for your part in it being possible…" She froze for a moment. Second chances. Second chances. What was it about that phrase that kept sticking in her mind?

"Well, it was good to see you. I am glad you are doing well. You are right, Jacob. The accent is quite charming."

"Oh, I forget about that. Ha… Thank you and have a good day." She had already began to turn away when she heard them retreating to the deli counter. Her mind had latched onto something. Second chances. What was it? The years of abuse made it hard to concentrate. She cursed herself. What was it? Yes! That is IT. How could she have forgotten it? It was there in her school. She was on the right path.

And, thanks to Dr. Kauffmann, she had found it. A name for *him*. Her favorite novel in high school. It was about a second chance at love. It could be her second chance at love and life as well. Jane Austin's Persuasion would be the source to answer her question. She tried it several times to see if it fit him. Fredrick. Fredrick. What was his last name? Wentworth. Yes… Fredrick Wentworth. It sounded a little stiff. She started to laugh. Yes, he could be quite stiff from time to time given the fits. Ha. Ironic. She continued to say it in her head and aloud. Fredrick. Freddie. Yes. It fit. Freddie was her second chance at everything. She began mopping. The task was finished. She repeated the name again and again so it was as familiar as his face in her head. Freddie. It all was so perfect that it had made her forget about the beautiful golden watch that had been so important before.

4

Annie hurried along the path home carrying her day's packages. She had clothes for him. No, she had clothes for *Freddie*. She made her way up the stairs and met the General in the hall.

"Annie."

"Evening General." She saluted him.

"Ah, well then. How is the soldier?"

"He is doing well, General. He is actually moving about more these days. I can't say as that he is talking much, ya know. But, it is getting better."

"Good. Well done. There have been no orders to evacuate him yet. So, carry on."

"Yes sir. Night General."

"Dismissed."

Annie hurried to his room. It was already getting dark. She unpacked his meal and went to the cot to prepare for her nightly routine of feeding and cleaning him. To her surprise, he was awake and looking at her.

"Hey there. Are ya hungry? I brought your supper. You must be ready because you are awake and waiting. Ok, we'll clean you up after."

Annie went to the cot and set up her post. She looked up and found that he had propped himself up waiting.

"Hey, you are starting to get about now aren't ya? Do you want to sit up?"

He made a low soft sound that Annie had come to understand as yes. She sat the food down and reached over and lifted him to sit up against the cracked wall. He seemed to struggle a little to keep his head up.

"Ok, you want to lie back down?"

Again, he responded with a much louder sound that was higher pitched than the first.

"Ok, that'd be a no. Ok then. Let's get something in the old stomach here and see how ya feel." Annie began to break the food up and heard the loud sound.

"What? You are really taking me for a loop today? Aren't you hungry?"

The low sound confirmed what she knew.

"Well, then what is it?"

He raised his hand and held it up as if to pause her.

"Ok, well love, we can wait. What is it?"

His hand slowly moved back. His finger touching his chest.

"What?" She looked into his eyes that seemed fixed upon hers. She was confused. She looked at him while he sat motionless in that pose.

"OH! No, I hadn't forgotten at all! I did find a name for ya. I told you I'd do it. I thought about it long and hard all day. I found one that is special like you. I hope you like it, I mean, I can find another if ya don't. It was just something special to me, ya know. Like you are to me. Well, yea, let me get to it then. I would like to call you… Freddie. Officially it would be Fredrick Wentworth, but I'd like to call you Freddie. You are my second chance, love. Maybe I am yours too. And the name is about a story of second chances. I think you and me, well, we need a second chance. What do you think?"

He continued to look in her eyes and his hand lowered from his chest. It reached to the edge of the cot upright. Annie took the hand he offered. That was it then. He would be her second chance. She smiled at him and returned to the meal. She talked to him referring to his new name as often as she could telling him about her day as she did each night. She talked to him about her past and what their future may hold. He sat there only to respond in his low pitched sound from time to time listening to her.

"You know, Freddie. I want to try to move you a bit more. You seem to be getting stronger. I'd like to move you more like your legs and arms – get them moving. I believe that you could walk since you have been moving about on your own. We are going to start trying that in the morning. Is that okay?"

A soft low sound responded.

"Good, cause I think you can do it. I don't know what happened to ya, but if we work together, well, maybe, right? I have to sleep now. Hey, I got a new watch. See it. It will help me get to work on time and back to see you on time now every day. We are a team you and me. I'll see ya in the morning Freddie." She laid him back on the cot and hesitated. She leaned forward and kissed his forehead. She hurried up to her room to get some rest and be ready for the morning's new routine.

Annie began each day going to the infirmary and slowly made progress at moving Freddie's extremities. They were sometimes limp like noodles and at other times stiffer than cement. She learned quickly that those stiff days seemed to result in more discomfort to both of them than the effort merited. So, they focused on days when Freddie's body would cooperate with them. It grew easier as the days, weeks and months passed by.

"Good morning, Freddie." Annie entered the dimly lit room and went to the cot. She leaned over and lightly kissed his forehead.

"Are you ready for our morning workout?" Annie positioned herself at the side of the cot.

"Ok, show me what you got this morning. I swear that we will be the fittest people on earth soon." She waited as his eyes focused and looked at her. The low, soft sound gave her the signal that he was ready to proceed.

"Ok, love. Then give it a go. The General has been asking to see your progress. I can't wait to show him." Annie waited while her patient prepared himself.

Annie sat waiting for the usual events. Freddie could now prop himself up and with minimal effort, move his sluggish limbs on his own. He tired quickly when they had started this but seemed to be getting stronger with each passing day. This particular morning, Freddie seemed especially alert. He had met her gaze as soon as she started speaking and watched her eyes while she prodded him to move.

Freddie slowly sat himself up. She helped him turn his body so that his feet were upon the floor.

"Good work there, Freddie. You are doing so well. Ok, then. I'll take over. Maybe today we'll pretend to dance again with those legs."

Annie waited for him to relax so she could move the legs to an imaginary beat that seemed to keep her amused with the task. But, he didn't relax.

"Hey, Freddie. I can't move your legs if you don't relax. Now, try so I can start." Again, the legs seemed stiff and heavy.

"Ok. Maybe you are having a bad day again. I'll try again when I come back this evening."

A loud sound stopped her from continuing with her thought.

"What?" Annie waited a moment. She looked at the tensed limbs and then back at the waiting eyes that never left her.

"Ok, you want me to try again?"

The same loud high pitched sound responded.

"Ok, well Freddie, I am going to be late to the deli. I can't stay here all morning waiting for your muscles to relax. Don't worry. It isn't a problem. We'll do it later."

Annie turned to get the water from the jugs along the wall. She would need to clean him up and give him something to drink and prepare to get to the deli on time. She carefully checked the golden watch that never left her wrist. Yes, she was still on time. She grabbed the bowl, rag, and cup and turned to go to the cot. The sound of the bowl hitting the floor was followed by the smaller sound of the cup doing the same. She stood there frozen.

"Freddie? How... did you... *get up?*" Her eyes were blinking at the figure of the man standing beside the cot.

Standing beside the cot. His eyes were fixed on hers. He did not move.

"Freddie... that is incredible. How did you... Have you been practicing while I have been away? There is no way you could have just, I mean... Freddie, *you are standing!*" Annie kept blinking to fully take in the sight. Yep, she thought, he is definitely standing. Annie moved toward him slowly.

She stood in front of him amazed that the slim figure was actually upright on its own. It was the first time she had seen him standing. He was taller than she had expected. And somehow, even more attractive than she had thought before. She stood very still and looked him over wondering how long he had been working on this without her knowledge.

"Is there any more surprises for me today? I think that one takes the cake! Are you tired? Do you need to sit?" She began to worry that he may fall and cause himself some harm that would set them back months. She thought it best to return him to the cot. She took a half step forward.

The silent man began to move. Annie feared he was starting to fall. Before she could reach him and put her arms out, he had taken a step toward her. Her mind was ticking. He not only stood, but he had just *walked.* She stood in front of him in disbelief. It almost seemed like a dream. It was worth being a little late to the deli. She allowed him to show her several steps forward as they stood there. She begged him to return to his cot so she could safely leave him until this evening. He silently complied.

Annie hurried along her daily route to the deli. She was only minutes late, but she wanted no reason for questions. She scooted into the deli as fast as possible.

"Good morning, Annie." I beat you here today. Mr. Berwitz was already behind the deli counter preparing.

"Ah, morning Mr. B. Yes, I guess even with the watch, people can still lose track of time. I am sorry about it."

"Ok, Annie. It was a few minutes. Don't worry about it. It was just odd not seeing you waiting when I got here. That is all. So? How are things?" Mr. Berwitz often enjoyed talking with Annie during the preparation phase of the morning. It passed the time and he was often amused at her slightly off-center take on things.

"Thank you. Um, things are fine." She disappeared into the back and reemerged with her bucket and rag to begin the tables and chairs. She began her familiar task but did not fill the quiet with her idle chatter. She was too consumed with the morning's events to talk much at all. She quietly worked as her mind churned on what had happened this morning. She wondered why she was feeling so at odds about it. It was a wonderful thing, wasn't it? Freddie had stood and walked to her. That was what they wanted, right? She scowled at the hand holding the rag. What was it?

Annie continued to attend to her chores without as much as a word. Mr. Berwitz became consumed with his tasks and the two worked simultaneously but in separate worlds. Annie kept wondering what the problem really was. She finally began to isolate the feelings to fish out what was nagging her mind. It wasn't that Freddie could stand or walk. It was that Freddie had been doing this while she was away. Surely this didn't happen overnight. What if he had fallen? What if he were injured? There would be no one there to help him. She could lose him. There was a risk now. She was completely invested in him. She felt the fear in her stomach at the thought of anything happening to him that seemed to reach from her feet to her ears when she thought of it. She looked down and realized that her hands were shaking. This wasn't about Freddie's progress. It was about the potential for loss. It was so confusing to want one thing but to be so fearful of it at the same time. She would discuss this with him tonight. Maybe he wouldn't ever fall? Or, maybe he wouldn't need to move around while she was away. She didn't know. She just knew that he was all she had and facing the idea of something happening to Freddie shook her to the bone.

Annie returned to the office building to find Freddie standing in the hall waiting. She felt sick for a few seconds until she could regain her composure. She put her hand to her forehead to steady herself.

"Freddie. What are you doing? Trying to give me a coronary? Bloody hell!" She marched over to him.

"Get back into your room." She grabbed his arm and led him back to the infirmary.

She pushed him toward the cot and he turned around to face her. His eyes met hers and they stood staring at each other for a few minutes. She was angry. She was afraid. She needed to think for a minute to sort this out but couldn't keep it all straight with those large brown eyes peering down into hers. It was so distracting. She turned her back to him and began to pace back and forth across the room.

She shouted inside her head to herself. Why was he doing this? Didn't he see what could happen? Was he crazy or maybe just trying to make her crazier? She huffed and puffed as she paced back and forth. A single thought made her stop moving. He hadn't left the building. He just stood at the door waiting for her. Why was she so angry? This was an infirmary, right? Not a prison. Was he merely her prisoner? A pet? So many questions, so many emotions. Good God. Was she doing to him what she feared *they* would do? Lock them up and throw away the key? Was she being selfish? She stared blankly at the wall. It was overwhelming. She couldn't do it anymore. She turned to face him. He had not moved. His eyes still fixed directly upon hers.

"Freddie." She said to him softly.

"Freddie. I am so sorry to have been so... *mean* to ya. You just scared me, that's all. It was all a surprise really. I have wanted you to walk more than anything, you know? And, I thought it would be a little at a time and you go and just spring it on me like that. I have thought about it all day. I wonder if you hid it from me or if you were just trying to surprise me. I don't know. It doesn't matter, I guess. It is what we've been working on. I should be glad and all... I guess I just worry. I am used to being there for ya and now you seem to be..." her voice trailed off.

"We need to work on things together and now that you seem to be up and about, I want to show you around. You are not my *prisoner* here. I don't know where ya came from but we'll just have to work together to see where we are going."

Annie took him around the office building and showed him all their rooms and the make-shift facilities. She figured that was enough for now as she was hoping he wouldn't go wandering around outside just yet. She was definitely going to have to warn the General about the new status of their soldier. He definitely didn't like surprises.

It was almost six o'clock. Annie was just finishing up filling and straightening the stock room at the deli. She was thankful that she could just stay at the deli all day now. She had liked going to the pier at six, but it kept her there until after eight o'clock. That left little time for Freddie. Mr. Stillman was good enough to continue his kindness to the General without her. They did really like him. So, it was a good arrangement. The General was well fed by the fishermen and she had her work at the deli that took care of Freddie and her. It was all working out so well. She was, for the first time in a long time, happy.

Annie made her way to the office building. She skipped up the steps and opened the door. Oddly, Freddie was not there waiting for her as he had been since the day he revealed he could walk. Definitely odd. Annie frowned and called out his name. No response. She stopped and instantly feared that maybe he had left the building. Her pace quickened as she went room to room looking for him.

Annie yanked the door to the infirmary open and saw Freddie lying upon the cot. He was not moving. She saw his stiffened body contorted into the small ball he became during these attacks. She began to walk toward the cot.

"Aw, Freddie. I see you are having one of your spells again. Let me sit with ya until this passes, ok. I brought your dinner. We will wait until it passes."

Annie sat next to the cot and heard a low groan begin to erupt from Freddie. It grew louder and more intense each minute. The sounds became more of a throaty growl that was almost impossible to identify as human sounds. She became more anxious as they seemed to intensify. Suddenly, Freddie's body began jerking back and forth on the small cot. The sounds were deafening. She feared he would fall from the cot and possibly hurt himself in the fall, but there was no way for her to grasp him now to get him to the floor. She watched helplessly as he thrashed upon the bed in an endless series of positions. Annie was horrified at the length of this attack. It had been more than two hours and it appeared the attack was slowing and she was able to get close to the cot without fear of being harmed by the flailing limbs.

"Freddie. Wow. Freddie. That was a bad one. Hey, how are ya? Let me get you into a more comfortable position here." Annie moved the semi-rigid body back into a lying position on the cot. She almost screamed when she reached to adjust his head. She stood there looking in horror. His eyes were blood red and there were several drops of blood coming from his nose and mouth.

"Oh my God, Freddie. What has happened?" She turned quickly to get her cloth and some water to clean him up.

"Freddie? Can you hear me? What *was* all that? I haven't ever seen ya go on like that before. I really don't know what to do, love. I will definitely talk to the General. He should be here any minute. Maybe he'll know what to do." Annie worked quickly now that Freddie was motionless and silent. He did not respond to her voice or her touch. She kept blinking to fight the tears she felt burning in her eyes.

"General? Is that you?" She heard the door close to the building.

"General?" Annie heard the rhythmic footsteps coming to the door. A loud knock followed.

"Yes, General. Please come in."

"Evening Annie. How is the soldier? I suppose he is talking now too! Ha ha ha."

"No, General. He isn't. He... well, he just began making the worst noise and shaking all about the cot. I've cleaned him up a bit, but look at him. He was bleeding from his nose and mouth and look at his eyes. General... what should we do?" Her words came out so fast that they were barely intelligible.

The General moved closer and squinted as he scanned the still body of his soldier. He lifted the eye lid of the closed eyes and saw the broken blood vessels hiding beneath them. He stepped back and paused.

"Annie, I think we are going to need some outside help with this one. I don't think HQ is going to send anyone in to help with this one. It must be too risky. So, we may have to find help on our own."

Annie looked at the General with wide eyes.

"But, Sir, you know what could happen. They could just take him away from us and we'd never see him again. Who could we trust here with him? I can't just watch him like this, but I am so afraid of taking him somewhere out there. I don't know what to do."

"You could be right. You never know where the enemy has infiltrated. We could go and see the men at the post near the mission. They have helped me before. I trust them. When the enemy got me with the biological weapons and I was sick, the men at the pier told me about these two. I went and they helped me right away. Good as new. We could try that."

"What? That is so far away and you see the shape he is in. Do you think we have to take him with us or could we just go and see if they can give us something for him?"

"Guess it wouldn't hurt to ask. Do you think we can leave him alone while we go? It is getting late. Best not for either of us to go it alone now. It's not safe. We would have to both go by subway. Fastest way there."

"Hmm... yes, I think we could. He is so still now and the fit has seemed to pass. We could hurry and see what your friends think. Let's go. It can't hurt."

"Ok. We are now on a mission. It is currently 2100 hours. We should be back in several hours if we are lucky and find the friendlies there at the post."

Annie and the General hurried the familiar path through the darkened streets being careful not to be noticed to the subway entrance. A quick scan showed some luck as the station was empty. Last train should be there in less than a half hour.

The subway train was on time and the two hopped on for the short ride. They exited and crept up from the stairs to the street.

"Alright. Looks like the coast is clear. Follow me."

Annie walked quietly behind the General. He took her to a side street just before the 16th Street Mission. It was several blocks and they came to a small fire station. The General walked quietly to the rear of the building to a small metal door and knocked softly.

Footsteps were approaching and Annie backed away from the door. She had no idea who may open it.

The door swung open and man peeked out.

"Who is it? Who is there?"

"Is that you Private Garcia?"

"Yes. General! How are you? It is a surprise to see you at our door again. Is something wrong?" The man exited the door and came out to greet the General, shaking his hand. He looked concerned.

"Yes, I am sad to say so. We need some help. I hate to bother you son, but it is urgent."

"Is there something wrong with you or your lady friend here?" Garcia was one of the two resident paramedics for the EMT vehicle housed at this fire department substation. He looked at Annie after visually checking the General for obvious injury.

"No, private. It is more about a wounded comrade. He wasn't well enough to make the trip. I thought Annie here could explain to you what happened and see what you think about it. Is there anything you can give us for him? I think it is quite bad."

"Sure, but you don't think you should have just called an ambulance?"

"Son, you know we can't trust just anybody with the enemy behind every corner. This is our only option."

"Ok, well, let's sit here on the bench and tell me what happened to your friend."

"Private Garcia, this is Annie. She is one of us. She has been caring for the wounded soldier for about a year now. He was making progress until today. Annie... tell him what happened."

Annie looked at the man and he had a kind face with big eyes that seemed to want to help. She was still a little afraid, but began telling him what had happened to Freddie this evening. She stopped herself for a moment. Focus.

Annie began to tell Mr. Garcia every detail of Freddie's symptoms from when she found him and his progress.

She was careful to describe today's events in every detail so maybe he could help.

Juan Garcia listened carefully to their story. When Annie finished, he was deep in thought. His first instinct was to tell them to go straight to an emergency room, but they had made it clear that they would not take that route. Sad that these people felt they couldn't trust anyone. And, whoever this poor sick friend of theirs was, well… truly was ill.

"Ok, Annie. It is really hard for me to diagnose your friend. You see, I am not really a *doctor*, and I don't have him here to at least do a routine check of his vitals, you know? So, it is pretty hard for me to say. Like I said before, the hospital is probably the best place to go."

"No." Annie shook her head violently at the thought.

"Ok, well, it appears your friend is suffering from some type of seizure disorder. He may have other problems as well that are keeping him from talking and moving properly. It could be a number of things really. It would be impossible to know. I can say that from your description of tonight's events, his situation is quite serious. Any seizure that violent to cause him to bleed from his nose and mouth are dangerous. They could even cause death if he has another. So, you both have to understand that this really serious."

Annie and the General stood silently looking at the ground in front of them. Neither moved or said a word.

"Ok, look. I happen to suffer from migraines and use Depakote for them. It is also an anti-seizure medication. I can give you some of them to try. It is dangerous for all of us to do this. First, we don't know how your friend will react and will not be able to check him for liver function and other potential side effects without regular doctor visits. Secondly, if anyone finds out about this, I am in really BIG trouble. Do you both understand?"

Annie and the General nodded in understanding.

"Ok, wait here. I really shouldn't be doing this, but I can't imagine what the poor man is going through. So, let's give it a try."

Garcia disappeared into the building and was gone for several minutes. He returned with an unmarked plastic container.

"Ok, I need the pill bottle to refill my prescription. I just refilled it so you have sixty pills here. Give him one per day and see if the seizures diminish or disappear."

Annie reached quickly for the medication in a determined hurry to get back to Freddie to try this medicine right away.

"Wait." Garcia pulled the container back.

"I can't give this to you without saying this. If these do not work and he continues to have seizures it could be very dangerous. I cannot examine him here. So, we are working in the dark. If he has another one like you described today, you will have to act quickly and decide what you want to do. He may not survive another major seizure. Do you understand?"

"Yes." Annie looked the kind man in the eyes and saw that he was worried.

"Sir, I'll take care to watch him and give him the medicine like you said. I won't tell a soul where it came from should anything happen. And, I will be sure to do something if one of these fits or seizures as you call them happens again. You have my promise."

Garcia handed Annie the container.

"Thank you sir. You are very kind to help us."

Garcia smiled and turned and went back inside the station to finish his shift. He wondered if he had done the right thing.

Annie and the General quickly made the long walk to the office building. There were no more subway cars running tonight and they would have to walk. Dangerous and time consuming.

Annie quickly rushed up the stairs to her building and went directly to Freddie. He was still on the cot not moving. She got some water and a single pill that she hoped would help him – help them both.

Several weeks passed. Annie was busy at her duties at the deli. She had been very anxious these past weeks. She was watching Freddie very closely in case the pills didn't work. He seemed to perk up a few days after the seizure and then several days later, had returned to his prior self. She was starting to feel optimistic that these pills were the answer she was looking for. Surely if the General went back there next month and told the man how they were working, he would give them more. Although she felt good, there was still some nagging doubt in her mind. What would she do if it happened again? She needed to have a plan this time. She decided that if it even looked like Freddie was going to have a seizure, she would take him to the fire substation right away. That way, Mr. Garcia could look at Freddie and see if there was anything more he could do. That would probably be the best thing. No hospitals. She had developed a plan and felt better than before. She was prepared for something she hoped would never happen again.

Annie hurried home with her usual assorted bags. Some had food, some had clothes and some had toiletries. The Berwitz were truly angels, Annie thought. She was anxious to see Freddie and tell him what she had decided today. She didn't like to keep things from him. Best he knows what to expect.

Annie entered the building and again, Freddie was not waiting for her. She went to his room and saw him sitting very still on the edge.

"Freddie. Hello. Why weren't at the door? Are ya tired today?"

Annie waited for his usual response. Nothing. His eyes were staring straight ahead.

"Freddie? What is it? Are you feeling okay?"

She knelt down in front of him and reached for his hand. She felt a slight tremor deep in his arm.

"Freddie? Is it happening again? I mean, you know. One of the seizures? Is that what is going on here?"

Annie clenched her eyes shut when she heard the fainted low sound come from him.

"Well, that is it then. Come on. Can you walk? We are going to that fire station Freddie. That man *has* to see you. He just *has* to see you so that we can find a way to help you. Freddie, can you walk?"

A low almost inaudible sound came from him. Annie knew if he was losing his ability to make sounds then the attack was not far off. She had to get going. It was still early. The tunnel would be full of people catching their nightly ride home. She thought a minute, but then looked at Freddie. His hand now was starting to show signs of visible shaking. She had to go now if she was going to go.

It had to be now or risk what the man said could actually kill him. She had a plan. She was going to stick to it.

"Get up Freddie. I need you to get up and come with me. I can't carry ya. So, you gotta walk. As fast as you can now. We got to get you someplace before this thing happens."

She grabbed his hand and pulled him out of the building and down the path. She was careful to keep an eye on Freddie and anyone they may encounter in the streets. It was terrifying. She felt almost naked outside with him like this. Her heart was racing as she pulled him along. She felt the arm she was holding begin to quiver.

"Hold on Freddie. We just got a little ways to go. I need you to fight this for me. Ok?"

As she talked to him, she also reminded herself to stay focused. Her mind was going in a million directions and it was hard to make quick decisions when she couldn't think. There it was – the subway entrance. It was only a block away. She was already pulling harder on Freddie's arm as he seemed to be walking more slowly than before.

5

*T*he tunnel *was* crowded today. During the commute it was almost a sea of bodies with a noise level that was a blend of individual voices that formed a deafening hum resounding inside the confined space. This was not a choice moment to move him. But, Annie saw the signs she knew so well. He was sinking into another major attack and there was no alternative. She had to get him to the fire station near the 16th street mission where they would surely, mercifully give her more or a different medication that the General explained might help pass this episode.

It was getting worse. He was now gnashing his teeth and the sounds now like a growling moan were coming from his throat and were getting louder. She was thankful for the noise drowning out his sounds. It wouldn't draw much attention in this environment. Although most people just ignored people like them... it was just always risky that someone *would* notice. That could mean trouble for them – too many questions and no easy answers. Annie was almost dragging him now as he seemed to be stiffening like curing cement.

It was tough getting through the throngs of people, but thankfully she was making progress and hoping to get the short distance to the exit before this got much worse. They were being shoved back and forth almost losing their footing while she struggled to keep him moving across the sea of people. His eyes were no longer visible as they were rolling upward under his lids. Annie knew there wasn't much time and decided to take the path closest to the tracks before she would lose the ability to pull him along and have to choose a place to ride out the attack.

The thought of that made Annie shudder... This was not an area where they had many safe places to hide. The attack could last a while and they were some distance from the office building. She just had to keep pulling him now in front of the lines of the crowd along the platform.

Just then, a surge forward from the crowd began as it neared the arrival of the next departure. As Annie struggled to maintain her footing, she lost her grasp upon Freddie's arm. She began yelling his name "Freddie! Freddie!" But her voice seemed to disappear in the loud noise of the crowd. She fought against the massive force pushing her further away from where she had lost him still screaming his name.

"Oh God, someone help me!" but it was only loud inside her shrieking mind, she knew that no one was listening. They had always been invisible to the outside world. Something no one wanted to see and now she was fighting to keep the only thing in her life that mattered – that gave her a purpose and a reason for living... Where *WAS* he in this sea of bodies as her arms and hands kept reaching between them to frantically feeling out his familiar, rigid body?

From about a distance of twenty-five feet she heard a blood curdling scream that froze her entire body. A sickening familiar growling tone in that scream shattered all her thoughts. And, then more of them followed as if it were a choir of sirens echoing through the tunnel rising in intensity being joined now by loud shouting that pounded inside her head along with her beating heart. WHAT WAS HAPPENING?!!! repeated in her mind until she found the ability to move again.

The force of the mass of bodies shifted and she found a small space to move between them and toward the source of the sounds. It was like a maze of backs and arms and hands but she kept pressing her body into them to reach… to reach *what* she didn't know, but to get to Freddie was all that mattered.

At last… she had pushed to the edge of the platform to see the source of the commotion. The contorted yet relaxed figure of the body was alien except for the recognition of the clothing it was wearing. It was *FREDDIE!* He lay motionless on the tracks and the smell of something burnt was pungent and sickening in the air. He was on the rails. Her mind slowly came to grasp the sight… "NO!" she screamed, "NO! NO! NO!"

As she tried to push forward to get to him, the weight of the mass changed direction and pushed her back. The police and rescue teams had arrived and she could see between the bodies the bright uniforms of the safety workers getting to Freddie. She struggled to move forward but it was impossible. She was forced back until she could no longer see the tracks, the rescuers, or Freddie.

Her mind raced stricken in panic. Was he dead? Where would they take him? How would she find him? How would she know if he survived? In either case, she knew that he had been lost. No one would help her. No one knew who he was to her. They didn't help people like her and Freddie. They were largely ignored and shuffled off to obscure places where no one had to see them. Alive or dead, she had lost him. Now gasping for air and Annie's mind spinning at a million miles per hour... It started very faintly until she could feel the tingling in her arms, legs and teeth. No, not again. It was the last thing she felt as the whole scene faded dark and she fainted amidst the chaos without anyone seeming to notice her – a tattered, crumpled rag to be stepped over upon the cold cement floor.

The rescue team reached the motionless body on the tracks. Several transit authority workers and police officers were already there pushing back the curious crowd and keeping anyone from interfering in the rescue effort. One of the officers yelled out to the rescue team. It was Kyle O'Rourke, immediately recognized by the majority of the team. Officer O'Rourke was assigned this beat many years ago and was often the first responder to any incident in his territory. His huge size was a great asset in this situation keeping onlookers away from the scene and giving the team the room they needed to work. The team instantly knew the chaos on the platform would be controlled and they could focus on their task.

The current had been shut down by subway workers. It was safe for the EMTs. They swiftly began to assess the situation. Mark Elliot had been an EMT for some fifteen years. His skills were practiced and thorough. He methodically crouched by the man lying on the rail. He began detailing the injuries and seeking any sign that signaled life. It was going to be difficult in this case. He signaled for the stretcher. He would act swiftly until he was sure there was no chance.

The man was face down and had apparently fell face up upon the highly charged rail. This was quickly noted by the acute burn that ran from the back of the head down the length of the back. The clothes had been charred leaving an open view of the long deep burn. There was minimal bleeding as it appeared the wound had been cauterized by the current. The smell of the burned flesh was intense and only momentarily allowed for a slight whiff of burned hair and clothing. Mark quickly reached under the man where his wrist would be to find any sign of hope this man had survived with little faith he would find it.

Mark's trained hand found the target. As he waited for some sign of a pulse, amazingly enough he felt a very slight shudder in the man's chest. It was enough. Mark began shouting "Let's go!" to the others signaling urgency and they responded. The team artfully braced the man's neck and limbs and whisked him to the waiting stretcher in one precise, fluid movement. While the others were securing the straps, Mark quickly radioed the nearest ER giving them the brief synopsis of the man's condition and an ETA. It would be a one-sided race. Death came so quickly while he had to depend on skill and a lot of luck in these cases. The team jogged the victim to the ambulance like Olympic athletes giving this one hundred percent of their physical abilities. He shot O'Rourke a glance and shook his head in the negative signaling the gravity of the situation. The officer nodded in understanding as they continued without missing a beat leaving him to disperse the crowd and gather the essential details for a report.

It seemed like moments took hours, but the screaming siren stopped and the team quickly assumed their positions and jetted into the awaiting trauma center. A rush of cool green garbed people surrounded them and a man stepped forward asking Mark for details. Mark gave the doctor what little information he had. They had not flipped the man over due to the extensive injuries on his head and back and left the man's face and any perceivable sign of life a mystery facing the clean white linen on the stretcher.

Mark watched as the green mass moved like precise machines transferring the man to their wheeled bed. Before he could study the man any further, they were running with the bed toward the double doors where all the life-saving equipment resided. "Would he make it?" he wondered aloud. Like the thousands before him, he knew he may never know. Just the memory of that deep burn which gave him a good idea of the probabilities here. "How did that happen?" he whispered to himself.

Well, if it were any consolation, O'Rourke had responded to this mess. His track record as a first responder was fairly good. Surely he'd have a pretty good idea of what transpired. Mark made a mental note to remember to ask him the next time he saw him. He stopped himself. It was not good to delve too deeply into why things happen.

He just had to concentrate on the fine efforts they made today and be satisfied. There were not always answers to the remaining questions in this job. Back to work. He had six more long hours left on the shift. Hopefully they would be less stressful than the last hour had been. He hopped back into the ambulance and cleared the incident with his dispatcher to wait the next moment he would be needed and forget about the unfortunate man he left in the hospital.

<h1 style="text-align:center">6</h1>

" **A**lright, alright. Listen up! It was an active night. So, we have a lot to get through today. Let's start with the high profile updates. Sanchez and Bello are on the recent homicide. Sanchez – any ID on the body from the pier?" The neatly uniformed man leaned on his podium waiting for his answer.

"Not yet, Captain. As you already know, he didn't have any kind of ID on him. We do have a lead that this guy was seen at the mission three days ago. We're going by there first thing today to talk with the workers and see if anyone has a story on him. We did get the coroner's initial report. Definitely gunshot wound as the cause of death. We sent the casing to the lab and are waiting for the results. Probably trying to rip off the dope man if he was at the mission." Detective Sanchez sat back down in his seat at the long table.

"Ok. Check with Vice for an MO and be sure to check the physical description with recent missing persons from the surrounding areas. He's definitely not a regular. Check outside the city. Next item. Detective Wallace. Where are you at on the string of robberies on the west end?"

"Morning Cap. I got several good witnesses. From the description so far, seems like it could be our old friend Andre." He's out again. Fits the description and MO. I got the witnesses coming in tomorrow to go through a photo lineup. If they pick him out, I got enough to get the warrants and get him in for a statement. If I play it right with a positive ID, he will probably give up the other guy and take a deal. The prosecutor's on board with it. Easy if I get an ID. If not, it may hang me up."

"Well that's just great. We are getting some bad press on that one. Speed it up. I'm getting tired of the calls on that one." The Captain pounded his fist to the wooden top in front of him looking at those seated facing him with a scowl.

"Yes sir." Wallace nodded.

"Detective Barr. You got anything yet on that check scam?"

"I'm going through the surveillance tapes now. They are really grainy and the camera position was bad at all three banks. No one ever changes the tapes. They use them over and over. I got a call in to the state lab to see if they can clear up the footage. The teller from PSF Bank thinks she can ID him if she sees him again. So, I am working with Wallace on a lineup of our recent parolees to see if she hits on anything."

"Doesn't anybody have any solved cases here? I am expecting *solved* cases. Get moving. Next. Here's the rundown from last night. Busy night. Your assignments are listed. It isn't going to get any better with the warmer weather. So, I expect some movement on these by the end of the week."

"Captain?"

"Yea, Detective Thomas?"

"Cap, I mean, I'm still working on the triple felonious assault from last Friday. I have about twenty-five witnesses coming in over the next two days. Ah, come on Cap. There is no way I can take this one too."

"Well, we have three on vacation this week and two sick calls. Everyone is getting dumped on, Detective Thomas."

"Well, says here that the guy might be *retarded* or something from O'Rouke's report. Can't the Family and Youth Crimes handle this? I am buried!"

"Lieutenant Brown. Can your guys handle this one?"

"Hey, Cap! My guys can *handle* any case. But, we are buried in runaways and sex crimes. This doesn't seem like it is really *ours*. No one is for sure about the victim here. He *is* an adult from the report. It should be the adult crimes unit's case with all due respect." Lt. Brown retorted his answer from the back of the room.

"Cap! O'Rourke says he's some kind of vagrant and there are witnesses that he seemed sick or disabled... I just can't take another one with the triple. This might get some media coverage. I don't want to explain why I haven't talked to anyone about it for a few more days. I got all these witnesses coming and there is no way I can go to the hospital today..." The detective was flailing his hands as he spoke.

"Stop crying Thomas. Alright. Brown. It is yours. Get some of your people on it and fish out if it was an accident or not. I'll consider reassigning it if there is any sign of intent here."

"Yes Captain." Lt. Brown coolly responded. He knew that the crap floated downhill.

"Alright ladies and gentlemen. That's it. Get to work and solve some of this shit already. I feel like we're looking for Jimmy Hoffa around here. I want closed cases!"

The room became a loud chorus of chatter as the detectives filed from the daily roll call room and back to their respective offices.

"Solitro and Harris." Lt. Brown called the two detectives to his office inside the Youth and Family Crime office. "Come in here."

The two detectives shared a brief glance. They knew what was about to come their way – the stuff that floats downhill. They walked into the tiny office and stood before the large desk.

"Yes, LT?"

"Alright. I know you guys are swamped on that last string of sexual assaults, but I gotta get this one off the desk. See what you can do with it." Lt. Brown shoved the papers toward Detective Harris.

"Oh, well Lt. Brown, I am going on vacation tomorrow. I got airline tickets and everything. Whoa. I mean. Lieutenant, there is no way I can cancel." The man backed two steps away from the stack of papers waiting in front of him.

"Just freaking great. Ben and Chuck have the gang fight at the park and Vince has the whole week tied up with the neighborhood watch presentations. God. I need six more bodies to keep up with this shit." Brown grumbled a few words under his breath.

"I got it." Mikey hesitantly mumbled.

"Mikey. Are you sure? I mean, John is going to be off for a week and you got to tie up those other kids on that serial molester. This might not be something for one officer. I think I'd rather have a team on it." The lieutenant wrinkled his nose at the detective standing in front of him.

"No, I got it. The child protective services workers are helping out with the other assaults. They are on those. I can work between the two. You know how long it takes them to interview with the drawings and dolls? Hell, I can solve this case before they can get to asking what happened. It's no sweat. Really, LT. I got it."

"You're a trooper, Mikey. Ok. You are it. But, I am going to need daily reports. You know they are going to stay up my ass all week to see if we are *handling* it or not. I'm not even sure if the guy is going to make it from the reports. If he starts swirling around the drain, I need to know right away."

"I *got* it. I know some of the staff at PSF ER. I can swing by there on my way home and probably have half the story before tonight. Other than that, nothing more than some interviews and waiting for some lab reports. Cake."

"Oh, I just remembered. O'Rourke is the reporting officer. Any problem with that?" The lieutenant raised a brow.

"Nope. Not an issue."

"Ok. You got it. Don't screw up. They will crucify you on this one, you know?"

"Yep. Just like all the rest of them. Really. I got it." There was some annoyance starting to show up now in the detective's voice.

"Ok. Mikey, I want a report in the morning."

"Ok."

The two detectives exited the small office into the deserted hallway.

"Mike. Really. I feel pretty bad about this. It is a holiday coming up and wait... damn... Didn't you have some party to go to?"

"John. Go. Have a good time. I am fine. I absolutely hate parties. And, for the last time, I GOT IT!"

"Ok Mike. Ok. You got it. I mean, nobody thinks you *can't* do it. It is just bullshit that you get stuck with it solo. That's all."

"Thanks for the vote of confidence. I'll bet you five bucks I solve it before you get back. Seven days."

"No way, Mike. Not taking that bet. You got too much of my money as it is. Ok, hitting the street on the location the victim described to get an address on the last of the sexual assaults. You got the interviews?"

"Yep."

"Ok. I'll call you if something good turns up. If not, notes will be in your slot and see you next week."

"Ok. Have a good fourth of July, John."

"You too Mike."

Mikey Solitro walked to the office to survive the next eight hours of interviews. It would be torture at best to talk about "good touch and bad touch" for what would seem an eternity. Maybe this assignment was a blessing. It may even be better than having to go to Dorthea's party tomorrow. Sure, Dorthea Reynolds was Mikey's best friend. But, there was no doubt she'd snuck in a plan to present a potential blind date that would be less than tactful. No, more like total discomfort. This was the perfect out. Mikey *had* to work and everyone knew that the job always came first. Maybe this could be a *good* thing – if there was such a thing.

———•◦•———

The halls were almost vacant except for a few of the night shift employees. The familiar hum of the machines seemed louder tonight than normal. Probably because it was late. Mikey walked the familiar path to the nurses' station. Empty. It was to be expected since it was late. A soft spongy sound of footsteps came from around the corner.

"May I help you?" The nurse padded around the desk and sat at the computer terminal.

"Yes ma'am. I am Detective Solitro. I am here to check on a patient – a John Doe that came in last night." Mikey held out a gold badge and ID card and the nurse scanned the items. It was not the usual hour that Mikey made these visits. Therefore the staff was not familiar with the officer. The day crew would have been a whole different reception.

"Ok, Detective. He is in bed 8B. I don't think this visit will do you much good though. He is critical and completely unresponsive."

"Ok, who is the attending physician?"

"That seems to be changing almost every several hours due to the nature of the injuries. I think that the final decision will be made tomorrow morning."

"Sounds good. Is the current attending doctor free now? I just need about five minutes and then I can come back in the morning."

"Sure, let me call him."

Mikey walked across the shiny floor and leaned against the wall holding the file. It would probably be a while since there had to be only one doctor on the floor making rounds over night. Tomorrow would be more productive, but it was possible to get through the preliminary phase of gathering information and prognosis."

"Detective?"

Mikey was startled from being so lost in thought.

"Uh… Doctor, good evening. I am Detective Solitro. I am here for the preliminary investigation on the John Doe case that came in yesterday. What can you tell me?"

"Hello Detective. Well, I can't tell you too much right now. The man is in pretty bad shape. We have had almost the entire staff review his charts and tests. He is a neurological mess. We induced a coma right away due to the extent of the injuries so you can't talk to him. Well, it may be easier to show you. Come on."

They walked down the hall and turned into a room that was almost alive with lights and sound due to all the machinery connected to the figure on the bed.

"It appears that when he fell, he landed on his back on the charged rail. He has a continuous, long, deep burn that runs from the back of his head straight down the spine. We honestly don't know how he survived. The injuries should have been fatal. But, the tests show that despite the damage, his nerves are somehow *functioning*. It is truly a mystery. The tests are just in the beginning stages. This is definitely a puzzle."

"Is that why he is lying face down?" Mikey looked at the bed and the body lying there that seemed to be mummified in gauze while connected like an octopus to eight machines.

"Yes, we are treating the burns right now. They are fairly severe. The biggest hurdle is getting him past the danger of infection. The wound is very large and deep. By then, we should be able to get a better idea of his neurological status. He is going to be critical for a while, but his vitals seem incredibly stable right now. It could change at any time, but given the extent of the injuries, he is doing quite well."

"Ok. I understand that they are going to assign a lead physician tomorrow. So, I'll come back in the morning and see how he is doing. Thank you, doctor."

"You're welcome. But, just to warn you, this one is going to take a while to sort out. Well, medically. I know your job is focused elsewhere. But, it may be a long time before you are able to get a final diagnosis on this one. We've just never seen anything quite like it before. I doubt the poor man will ever function after this. There is just so much damage. He may spend the rest of his life in a vegetative state. So, good luck with your investigation."

"Thanks. Have a good night."

Mikey drove home making a mental plan of where to start on this case. Surely after the hospital, it would be good to go to the scene to get a visual image of where this all happened. Then, back to interviewing witnesses. O'Rourke was always thorough. There had to be at least eight listed readily in the report. This was going to be a lot of paperwork. Probably for nothing. It was always tough when you had no victim to talk to for clarification of such sketchy details. Hell, this may not even be a crime. Mikey sighed. This was going to be a long week. Just then, Mikey remembered the party. Yes, the first thing to do upon getting home was to call Dorthea. It would take the best acting to fake despair in having to cancel. Mikey smiled, pulled into the driveway and prepared for the Academy Awards.

"Hello?"

"Hey. It's Mikey. How's it going?"

"Pretty good. I have a few of the girls from work here. We are going over the list and any last minute details. I am so excited. This is going to be a great party and a great Fourth of July. You are going to be impressed, Mike. And, you might even have *fun!*"

"Yea, well... Dot... That's the reason I was calling. I...

"Mike! Do not tell me you are not coming. You always do this. You always back out on me. Now, you are my best friend. I do not want to hear nothing about you not coming. I mean, come on. After that crap with K..., you know who. You just crawled into some kind of hole. You gotta get out and meet people. This will be fun. So, don't say it."

Mikey's hand was tense and gripping the phone way too hard.

"Look, I'm sorry. I got stuck with a case today. John's on vacation and I've got to run it down by myself. I am sure you saw it on the news. The one where the guy ended up frying on the subway rail. So, I'm going to be working double on this one for at least a week. I know you're mad. But, what do you want me to do, Dot?" There were a few moments of silence.

"I'm sorry. I just really wanted you to be here. I don't see you as much as before and you just don't seem happy. We never just hang out. Now you're ditching on my party."

"Dot, I am not ditching. I have *got* to work this weekend. Hey, when John comes back, let's plan an evening together. Really. I'm going to need a night out. We could grab some dinner and a couple of drinks. I'll call you Monday and we'll plan something. Don't be mad."

"You owe me Mikey. I was only having this party trying to get you out of that house and mingling again. Oh, and you definitely got to tell me what is up with that guy. It was so crazy on the news. That poor man. Do you think someone pushed him or did he fall?"

"Too soon to tell."

"Is he going to live?"

"Looks like it. If that is what you want to call it. I guess he is really burned up. They aren't sure that he'll function if he recovers."

"Oh, I don't know how you do this shit. That is terrible. Well, I have to go. They are changing the appetizer list and I am not having that. I'll talk to you Monday. Have a good holiday."

"You too, Dot. Night."

That wasn't too bad. Mikey grabbed clothes for the next morning from the closet. The image of the mummified man reappeared along with the faces of all the children on the list of things to do tomorrow. Mike sat on the bed for a moment and got up and poured a glass of whiskey. Returning to the bed, the images kept turning around and around like a rubix cube until sleep finally came to stop the day's torture.

Mikey awoke early and began sorting the day's tasks into order of priority. It was going to be a long one. As soon as roll call was over, the hospital was the first stop. The rape case was ready for typing and after that it could be delivered to the prosecutor's office. Mikey winced. It was definitely going to be a long day.

Thankfully the roll call was short and uneventful. Mikey arrived at the hospital at nine o'clock. The halls were bustling with activity. This was the hospital that Mikey knew.

"Mikey!"

"Hey! Kim. I am glad to see you. I am here on a case. You got a minute?"

"Sure. Ha." Kim Lee, RN rolled her eyes.

"Yea, I know. Me too. Busy as hell. Hey, that John Doe from the other day… Did they assign a doctor?"

"Yea. I think it is Dr. Kauffmann. The worst part is the guy is indigent. So, they couldn't get anyone from either of the cities to come out here as an on-call specialist. You know… no money, no specialist. So, Dr. Kauffmann volunteered for it. He is such a nice man. So, that is who you are looking for."

"Wow. Why does that shit still surprise me? Anyway, thanks Kim." Mikey walked toward the nurses' station thinking it was always about the money.

"Yes. Hi, Arlena. I am here to see Dr. Kauffmann."

"Hi Detective. I think he is in with a patient. Do you have time to wait?"

"Yes, ma'am. I have all day." Mikey laughed.

"Okay. I'll try to catch him before he goes in with someone else for you."

"Thanks Arlena."

Mikey went and sat on the window ledge in the waiting room, lost in thought.

"Detective, the doctor can see you for a few minutes now."

"Thanks." Mikey walked down the hall to room 8B.

"Hello, Dr. Kauffmann?"

"Uh, yes… Are you the *Detective?*"

"Yes sir. I am." Mikey felt the doctor looking at – no more of an assessment of…

"Well, Detective. I am sorry. I was just expecting… well.. a…

"A what?" The same old statement that had been made a thousand times. Mikey unconsciously stood a little taller.

"Well, a *man*. Ha ha. I am sorry. They said detective and then someone said Mike. I just *assumed* you were a man."

Mikey's hands were clenched in fists. It was amazing this thing still managed to annoy her.

"Nope. And, for the record… It's Michela Solitro. The staff here knows me and uses my nickname." Mikey stood stiff and tall and stared directly into the doctor's eyes without blinking or moving.

"I see that, well… what can I do for you, Detective?"

"I am here about John Doe. I was here last night and there wasn't much they could tell me. I am investigating the incident to see if there is any criminal element involved. Aside from the obvious injuries, were there any secondary injuries that would indicate any sign of struggle?" Mikey was still annoyed and wanted to get to the relevant details so not to prolong the visit.

"No, we have gone over his entire anatomy. There were no secondary contusions or lacerations that indicated that. Obviously I can't rule it out, but at least there are no signs of it."

"Okay. What can you tell me about his current injuries and prognosis?"

"Well, that is a little more complicated. The tests just came back this morning. It had confounded everyone that he was not only alive, but was responding to neurologic testing. Any normal person would not have had any ability for a response due to the nature of the injuries. Follow me…"

They walked to the doctor's office. He pulled a large brown envelope from the top of his desk and put it on a lit clipped display on the wall.

"You see here? This is his MRI. The nerve trunk would have been where the dark wide line from the injury is. In his case, you can see the haphazard lines running through his midsection. It appears that the injury actually may have *solved* a preexisting condition – possibly a case of Spina Bifida. I'm not sure. None of his neurologic centers is where they are supposed to be and it appears were not in connection with each other prior to the accident. Where the electricity cauterized his body, it was like welding many of these randomly unattached nerves together. They are firing across the scarring wound where there was previously no connectivity.

Mikey looked intently on the lit film squinting into the lighted frame.

"How could that have happened?"

"We really don't know. I guess in plain English, this would - should have destroyed his entire nervous system if he had been a normal person. But, instead, it seems to have… almost… *repaired it.*" Dr. Kauffmann shook his head and walked to the light switch turning on the fluorescent light.

"There is still so much we don't know. There could be residual damage to the tissue rendering muscles useless or even the chance that this *repair* is temporary due to the inflammation at the site of the wound. We really don't know. I have assembled a local team and we will be watching and testing him at every turn to see what is going to happen here. It is really quite amazing. So, I hope that helps you. It is all we know right now. We will keep him in a coma until the burns heal and then see where it all takes us from there. I can't make any further guesses at this time."

"How long could that take? I mean the coma part."

"Maybe three to five weeks is my best guess."

"Ok. Thank you, Dr. Kauffmann. I have plenty to do on this case outside of the hospital. I will start there then and check in every few days to see how he is progressing. It may give me an opportunity to piece it together and then, by some miracle, he is able to talk, I can finish up here."

"Yes, I would say that this is nothing short of a miracle already. I don't have high hopes that our John Doe will recover fully. But, we will give him our best shot. I guess miracles do happen." The doctor looked at Mikey and noticed that the stiff cold exterior he first noticed had softened some. He even saw what looked to be the pain of understanding in the soft brown eyes of the dark haired woman looking at the films. She was so small. It was still hard to believe that she was a detective.

"Well, for his sake, I hope so. Thanks again, Doctor."

Mikey left the hospital feeling somewhat dark. Sad even. It was bad enough that some poor person had to endure this tragedy. But, to think that it was some challenged person who had probably already endured a ton of hardship... then to face this. The second thing that bothered her is that when she checked with hospital security after her visit with the doctor, they had nothing to add. He was brought in and they found no identification. Actually he had nothing in his pockets. No money. No papers. Nothing. And, they noted that no one had come in asking about him. It just didn't seem right. No relatives or caretakers? Nor did this seem fair. But then, life never really was fair at all was it? Mikey began thinking of some of her most recent victims. They didn't ask to be chosen. They were just at the wrong place at the wrong time and suffered the consequences. She shook her head hard and fast as if to stop the thoughts. Okay. It was time to go back to the office and attempt to get a game plan on the witness list. Hopefully one of these people could provide some of the answers to the million questions she still had surrounding John Doe.

7

"*H*ey Mike. So, how was last week? Did you miss me?"

Mikey looked up from her desk and saw John's big smile. She couldn't believe it had been a week. It seemed longer.

"Hey John. How was the vacation?"

"Great. Too short and too expensive. But, the wife and kids had a great time and I needed the break. So? Catch me up before the lieutenant sees me and I don't have any answers."

Mikey laughed. That was the truth. He couldn't wait until the chair was warm to start. He'd especially be anxious to have John back to help with the John Doe case.

"Okay. Well, the serial perv case has been submitted and the warrants have been issued. Just waiting for a tip on the guys whereabouts and that one is in the can. The lab results came back a positive match on a CODIS hit from the victims examinations. So, the DNA is a match. That will be an easy plea and one *solved* to report to the captain. We got a new one. Looks like a stinker. The victim's story keeps changing and I think there is more evidence to disprove the case than there is to prove it. I hate those false reports. And, then there is the ongoing case with John Doe."

Mikey looked down at her desk frowning.

"Well, you said you'd have it solved by now, so give me the scoop."

"Well, that was one bet you *should* have taken. I got zero."

"What? How do you have zero? Haven't you talked to people or the guy or what?"

John was actually shocked that there was no progress. Great. This could damage their reputation within the department. It could do more damage to his than hers since they didn't think much of her anyway. What had she been doing while he was gone? He started shaking his head.

"Look. I went to the hospital. He is being kept in a coma while recovering from the injuries. Then, he had nothing on him to get any leads. Ok, so I have been to the mission and no one there remembers ever seeing the guy. I interviewed all the listed witnesses. They really didn't notice the guy until he was on the rails. One lady thinks she saw him with a female just before it all happened. She recalled the woman having red hair, but then wasn't sure. She thought that they looked like vagrants. But, when I checked with a few of the people I know down in that area, no one seems to have ever seen the guy before. So, I have started checking all the missing adult entries to see if anything fits his description. Maybe he is a walk-away from some place further out that would keep us from making the connection. Hell, I don't know."

"Damn. Did you print him?"

"No, not yet. He is not in any condition for that yet, but I should be able to do it in a couple of weeks. John, I am running out of ideas here. And, as usual, my head is on the chopping block on this one. The captain has made it clear that I am solely responsible for the outcome on this one. So, keep your distance or you'll be on the block with me."

"Hey, Mike. We are partners. We'll figure it out."

"No, seriously. I think it would be best if you let me drown solo on this one. At least on paper. Maybe you could squeeze the victim on the bogus rape and it would sure free me up to keep my feet on the ground with this one. Hell, if I take a hit on it, at least we won't be behind on the rest of the stuff while I ride out the suspension!"

"You are a hard-head Mike. But, as you wish. I am not in the mood to get reamed my first day back. So I'll get on the other one and whatever comes in today. I'll run some interference with the LT for you. Go ahead out now. Just keep me posted so we are on the same page."

"Okay, Thanks John. Wish me luck."

Mikey hurried out from behind the desk and made her exit into the police garage. She hopped into her unmarked cruiser and headed toward the subway station. There were several ideas left. Mikey decided to get the most unpleasant one over with first. She listened to the police radio for five or six minutes and heard the voice she was looking for.

"Radio, log me out on signal eight next to the 16th street mission."

It was time to go and see Kyle for the first-hand details. Maybe there was something that was overlooked. Mikey parked about a block away from the mission and began walking looking for the familiar markings of a uniform in the midst of the people coming and going from the building. There was a commotion coming from the lot next to the building. Yep, she squinted and saw the person she was looking for. It appeared he had several people out of a car in the lot.

"Look ma'am. I saw you pull in here driving this vehicle with that expired plate. So, you can save the excuses and attitude for the judge. And, yes, you can call the mayor if you like. He should be in until four o'clock." The officer turned to leave and stopped upon seeing Mikey behind him waiting.

"Michela. I am surprised to see you out here. Are you lost?" He gave her an icy stare and began to walk away.

"Kyle, I am actually here to talk to you. Can I have a minute?"

"Talk to me about what?" He stopped and glared at her.

"Look, I am running out of leads on that subway incident. I was hoping that maybe something could provide me with more direction or something we overlooked. Do you mind going over it again?"

"It is all in the report. I don't overlook anything. If you don't have any leads, that is your problem. I can't believe that you are working on this one anyway. What? Did the whole detective division go on vacation? Leave it to the kiddy cops to mess this one up."

"Okay, you can still hate me. But I am serious. I need you to just go over it with me one time. You know I wouldn't be here if I had any other lead. Humor me."

O'Rourke rolled his eyes. He began telling the story and it was exactly what had been written on the report minus the names and specifics.

"OKAY? Is that it?"

"Yea, I guess so. I was just hoping that you could tell me something more. I am looking for anything I missed."

"Look, Michela. It was crowded. There were people everywhere. It was hard enough to keep the people from running toward the exit in a stampede once I got there. And, to make things worse, some homeless lady decides to pass out. We had to practically carry her out of the station. She came to and ran off before I could even ID her. It was a mad house. You are lucky I gave you what I did. That's it. There is nothing more I can tell you. If you can't solve it, that is *your* problem."

Mikey tilted her head and rolled her eyes.

" Thank you for your time. And, for the record, Kyle… It has been almost five years now. Get over it already."

Mikey turned and walked back to her car as she heard him spout out one last obscenity. At least she could say that she had spoken to the reporting officer. Thankfully she didn't have to detail the conversation. What an asshole. She remembered that there was a time that she and Kyle were crazy about each other. That seemed like another lifetime. When they split up, their secret was out and the no fraternizing rule had been broken. Kyle was transferred from the East end beat where Mikey was working to the West end beat. The West end contained the mission, the pier and the subway – all the places that produced most of the crime and work. It was a permanent punishment after all his years of service. That beat was usually reserved for the new officers and the screw-ups. It added insult to injury and he had always hated her for that. He didn't realize the punishment she had received in the constant belittling she endured daily. She definitely got hers too.

Mikey shook her head to refocus on the matter at hand. With that unpleasant task taken care of, she needed to move on. The next best thing would be to start in the center of the city and work toward the pier. It could take days, but going business to business may be the only way to draw out *someone* who had seen this man before the accident and know who he had been with and lead her to how he had come. She grabbed a large stack of business cards and began walking. Each doorway she encountered along the main street yielded the same result. She described the man and the people inside would claim they had not seen anyone matching that description around the neighborhood. It replayed over and over again. She left her card with each contact hoping that someone may remember something that would help. She left her card in doors where there was no answer. She was hot and it was getting dark. She had stopped at every business and apartment building from the central district to the pier. Mikey began walking back to the car she had left in the town center. She decided to stop at the hospital to see how John Doe was doing on the way home.

The hospital was much the same as she remembered it on her first day on this case. It was getting late and the halls were mostly deserted on the floor. She approached the desk to find the same older blonde nurse from that night.

"Hello again." Mikey smiled at the woman. "I suppose you know who I am here to see."

"Yes, Detective. He is still in room 8B. The doctor is unavailable. We had few new patients come in today. I am sorry."

"No problem. Do you mind if I go in anyway. I'll just spend a few minutes and be on my way."

"Sure. No one visits him. It would be nice not to see him in there alone." The nurse waved her hand toward the room.

"Thanks." Mikey walked the hall to the familiar room. She hadn't been there for several days. Some of the machines had been removed and it was less like a discotheque and more peaceful. She sat in the chair next to the bed in the dim light. She noticed that he had been turned over and was lying face up for the first time. She stood up and went to the bed and looked at the man's face. He was a little cartoon-like. His face seemed distorted and Mikey assumed this could have been swelling. His face was blank, expressionless. She noted his longer dark hair. His arms were thin and ended with square hands with long fingers.

"Hey. I am having a rough day and just wanted to sit with you for a minute." Her voice was warm but soft so that it couldn't be heard outside of the room.

"It is nice to finally see you today. I have been coming here for a while and now finally I know what you actually look like. I am really trying hard to figure out who you are and what happened to you. I am going to try not to let you down." Mikey reached her hand hesitantly to the arm lying on the bed. She gently touched the top of the hand and held it for a minute.

"I wish you could talk to me. Keep fighting, buddy. I am praying for you." She released the hand and exited the room and waved to the nurse. She was ready to go home. Tomorrow was another day. Maybe she could go to the pier in the late afternoon when the boats returned. It was something else to try at least. Yes. She could try that. And, she could possibly fingerprint the man now. Well, with the doctor's permission. She would focus on those two things tomorrow.

———◆———

Four weeks had passed since she was assigned the case in the subway. Mikey had submitted the man's prints to the State lab for a trace. She had interviewed all identified witnesses and canvassed every street on the West end. She had scoured the statewide system for missing adults and no matches were found. All she could do now was wait for the print trace or one of the contacts to remember something. The lieutenant was given constant updates during the first few weeks. The pressure to *solve* this one seemed to have subsided. It was a long standing but often unaccepted notion that *all* cases are not crimes and that *all* crimes cannot be solved. At least the efforts she made were well documented and in order.

Mikey knew she could probably safely close the case. There was no evidence of a crime and the case could sit in the pending files until something new came in. But, she had grown to look forward to her visits to the hospital. It was so quiet there now with most of the machines gone. She seemed to be comfortable now being there talking about her day while holding the hand of a stranger.

Doctor Kauffmann said that they should be eliminating the coma-inducing drugs any day. Mikey wondered what would happen. She just couldn't close the case just yet. She wanted to know if he would wake up. Maybe then he could answer all the questions about him that had puzzled her for all these weeks. She realized this was probably wishful thinking. No, definitely wishful thinking since the prognosis for that outcome was unlikely.

Mikey went to the familiar nurses' station on the floor to see John Doe. The same nurse was sitting behind the desk looked up and smiled.

"Hi Mikey."

"Hey Sarah. Just here for my nightly visit. Is that okay?"

"Sure. I think they are going to take him off all the meds and support tomorrow. I hope he makes it."

"Wow. What time are they doing that?"

"I'm not sure. But it will be during the day shift for sure when Dr. Kauffmann is here."

"Ok. Hey, thanks for letting me know Sarah. I really want to be here. It is his big day. I just don't know if I can handle it if... "

"*You* don't think you can *handle it*? Ha ha ha. For goodness sake, you are a detective."

"Yea, I guess I am. Ok, I am just going to sit with him a while and I'll let myself out if you are on rounds. Thanks again."

"Night Mikey."

She walked the familiar path to 8B. It looked the same as always, but tonight felt a little different. Mikey felt tense instead of relieved sitting in the chair. She was accustomed to talking in her warm soft voice now. It was automatic with him.

"Hey. It's me, Mikey. How are you doing today? I just heard the news. They are going to take you off all of the… well… stuff tomorrow. That's pretty great. That must mean you are doing better. It is good that one of us is doing better. I am still about the same. I still haven't really found out anything about you. I am really sorry. But, you know, it feels like I do know you. I have been trying and I am still not going to give up. There are just a few things I'd like to tell you tonight, well before everything tomorrow…" Mikey got up and reached for his hand.

"I am just really frustrated. I was sort of hoping that when they take you off all this stuff, that you are going to talk to me. I am sort of counting on that. So, I hope you are going to try really hard tomorrow. I'd really like that. I almost feel embarrassed to tell you that I am a little afraid. Well, and selfish. I have really come to look forward to visiting you. I may know how you feel. I know what it feels like for nothing to show on the outside. And, sometimes what it feels like to feel nothing on the inside. All these people who think they *see* me every day. Well, they really don't see *me*. They just see the shell. They don't see me at all. So, I think we are a lot alike. I don't think they really see you either. Just the shell sitting here. But, I want you to know that I *do* see you. Somehow I see that there is much more than just the body lying on this cot. I don't know why. It is just something in my gut. So, I am a little afraid of what is going to happen tomorrow. I don't think that I can handle being here when all this happens. I really can't imagine not coming here and seeing you every night after work giving me something to look forward to. I have never been good with people. But, I have felt really good here with you, John Doe. I gave them my cell phone number to let me know what happens. So, this is it. Thank you. I hope to get good news for your sake. Please live. Good night."

Mikey was fighting tears and gently squeezed the hand she was holding. She felt sad, confused and angry. She quickly walked the hall and then out of the hospital. She got in her car and sped home before the tears could overwhelm her ability to drive. She almost ran into the house and once inside burst into a wall of tears. She spent the first ten minutes sobbing just inside the door. Ok, Mikey. Get ahold of yourself. She went to the bathroom to wash her face and change her clothes. She got into the bed and began to think. God, was she that crazy that she had befriended some comatose man she didn't even know? How sad her life must be to have no other outlet than to talk to the quasi-dead. She laughed until she cried again. She meant every word she told him, but she felt guilty that she had used this unfortunate soul as a sounding board for her own misery and loneliness. She got up and poured a quick glass of adult beverage. She didn't want to think any more. Tomorrow would come. And, she would have to face the probabilities that John Doe would either not survive or remain in a vegetative state. Why was this hurting so much? She had watched people die, seen dead bodies, and heard the horror of atrocities beyond most people's wildest dreams. It was just another case. God, she was losing her edge and going soft. Something no one would believe. Something that she had been able to keep a secret even from herself until now. She did *feel* inside the cold exterior that the world saw.

Mikey began sobbing until she could barely breathe. That's enough she told herself. She would push this all out of her mind and forget about John Doe and the gaping hole she continuously hid inside her chest. She downed the whole glass of amber liquid and turned out the light. Tomorrow was just another day. Nothing more. No hopes. No dreams. No magical escape from this life. Just cases and the need to follow their logical order. She was again in control. Cold and unfeeling. Bring it on. She was ready for sleep and another mechanical day. Mikey allowed the haze of alcohol to carry her off to dreamless sleep. A safe place for someone like her where it all shut off like a light switch.

8

"*H*arris and Solitro! I need an update on the latest abduction."

"Well, Captain. We have issued an Amber Alert. In all probability, this is no stranger abduction. We have reason to believe that this is more of a custody battle in disguise. Dad has been showing signs of wanting involvement and we have been unable to get a bead on his whereabouts. So, we are keeping our options open with this one."

Ok, Harris. Keep me updated. Press is having a field day again on this one. And, what about the subway thing?"

"Well, after an extensive investigation by Detective Solitro, there is no evidence of foul play. No one saw anything that would give us any probable cause. It seems like an unfortunate accident. We have left the case open just to get an ID on the guy. But, the criminal aspects seem done."

"Ok Harris. Good work. Let's consider it closed unless something else turns up. File it."

"Ok. Thanks Captain."

John turned to look at Mikey with a big grin. One less file on their desk.

Mikey blankly looked away and stared at the wall behind the Captain. That was it. Case closed… and without any crap about it being *solved*. Imagine that. Mikey shook her head.

The roll call ended and the detectives filed out in their usual routine.

"Hey Mikey, what's up with the attitude? Is something wrong?""

"Nope."

"Well, are you pissed off or something?"

"Nope."

"Ok. Well, are you going to tell me why you are acting like this?"

"Acting like what?"

"I don't know. Just like you aren't there. You look like a statue." Do you feel okay?"

"I feel great. What's on the list for today?"

"*Ok!* Well, there is a court hearing at eleven o'clock and two interviews. One at ten thirty and one at eleven. Which do you want?"

"I don't care."

"Ok, well, I hate the interviews, so I'll catch the court. Is that okay?"

"Fine."

"You really okay Mike?"

"Yep."

"Okay. I am going to go get the file for court. See you after lunch."

"Okay." Mikey sat at her desk. She barely moved except to breathe and blink occasionally. This day would be long, but it would pass as long as she stayed within the protective walls that kept the world out.

Mikey maintained her robotic persona for the entire day. She managed it again for the next day and then the next. It was getting easier to do as each day passed. She performed her tasks without a flaw. She was able to put on the plastic mask for each interview or contact. The smooth smile and velvet voice that were so easy now after all these years to switch on as needed.

This was autopilot. And, it was familiar. She had been doing it for more than five years. She just somehow got caught up in some emotional garbage and was now back in control of it all.

Mikey managed to keep busy and the day seemed to go by. Slowly, but it went. And, so did the next day and the next. After a week she had returned to her previous clay figure that could not be shaken. She didn't blink at the parade of people that came and went. She prepared each file objectively with logic and fact. She kept thinking, only ten more years to get through until retirement. That was the goal.

"Hey Mike. Nice job on that last one! I totally believed that woman. How did you know she was lying? That was great. You totally twisted her up on that second interview. I even think the LT noticed that one. No one likes a false rape charge."

"I don't know. It just didn't make sense. Lucky. That's all. So, where are we on the abduction?" Mikey smirked.

"Oh, yea. Well, I located dad and served the search warrant with Wallace and O'Rourke. sure enough. We found the kid in an upstairs bedroom. I canceled the

Amber Alert and we got him on some custody charges. Case closed."

"Great. Our stack is getting smaller. We may catch up by the time we retire. So, I am out of here. Have a good night and see you in the morning."

"Ok, Night Mike."

Mikey walked to the garage and slid into the familiar seat. She looked at her cell phone and saw three missed calls from Dorthea. Shit. It had been over a month since she promised to go out with her after missing her party. Ugh. She deleted the messages. She knew what they would say. She stopped to grab something at the Chinese carry out and planned to call it an evening when her phone rang. The number was not familiar. Mikey hesitated to answer it. God only knows who it could be. Telemarketer. Great.

"Hello."

"Yes, may I speak to Detective Solitro?"

"Speaking." Mikey wondered who would have this private number.

"Hello, I am Addison O'Neill. I am a social worker at Porto San Francesco Hospital. Can I have a moment of your time?"

Mikey pulled over and put the car in park. She winced trying not to remember the most likely nature of the call.

"Detective?"

"Yes. What can I do for you?"

"Well, I have been assigned to the case of John Doe. I understand you are the investigator on the case. Well, there have been some developments. Well, definitely some developments. And, I was wondering if I could meet with you. I know it may be a little late, but the nature of this case seemed to override waiting until tomorrow. Can you come to the hospital?"

Mikey sat there unprepared for this news. Oh God. Were they going to tell her he had died. She knew they wouldn't do it over the phone. They wouldn't give any real details over the phone. They needed an in-person ID check due to HIPAA rules. Great. Cold Chinese for dinner.

"Sure. I am on my way. Ten minutes."

"Thanks Detective. I really need to talk to you."

Mikey pulled into the parking deck and badged the attendant. She walked into the information area and asked for the social worker. The clerk directed her down a long hall to a waiting area. Great. They were going to make her wait. She concentratred on taking deep breaths.

"Detective?"

"Yes."

"I am Addison O'Neill. Please come in."

Mikey mechanically rose from the chair and went to the office and stood until directed to sit. She had fortified the inner walls in the ten minutes it took to call her in here. She felt nothing.

"Detective. Please bear with me. Um, it has been an unusual few days. Anyway. I would like to talk to you about John Doe."

"Ok. Has he… died?"

"No! Not at all. He is actually doing… well… *well!*"

"You're kidding?"

"No, he has actually surprised the heck out of the medical staff here. When they stopped giving him the drugs to induce the coma, he waivered for the first six hours or so and after that, it has been straight uphill. No one can believe it really."

"That's great. So, why do you need to see me?"

"Well, it's just that several days after they unhooked him, he began *speaking*. Not a lot or anything. Just one word. Over and over actually. It has been driving everyone a little crazy."

"What word is that?"

"Mikey."

"*What?*"

"Yes, it's a little strange, but that is all he says. 'Mikey.' We couldn't even make it out at first. Then, we thought it was *his* first name, but when we tried calling him that he became agitated to the point we had to sedate him. The only thing the staff could come up with was you. Some of the nurses knew right away that Mikey could be *you*. They said it was your nickname and everyone here that knows you, knows you by it. And, you had been working on the case… So, I wanted to try it. It is all I have to go on. He just keeps saying it."

"What do you want from me?"

"Look, Detective. I can't make you do anything. I just was curious if there was a connection for his sake. I would like to ask you to *see* him. It would sure clear up some things. Maybe he even has information for you in the case. If there is no response then we will carry on the plan for rehab. It is just so gut wrenching to watch him call out this name and not be able to console him.… Do you see what I am saying? I would just like you to see him."

Little did this woman know that when Mikey laid down each night to sleep, she did see him. She kept seeing him. Mikey felt her heart begin to race and the solid walls she had built around herself were beginning to crack. She was working on keeping the panic unnoticed.

"Will you see him?"

"I don't know. I need a few moments to think about it. Could you leave me for a few and let me think? The case is closed now. I'm not sure what help I can be and I am not even sure of the propriety of the whole thing. Please I just need a moment and I'll let you know."

Mikey got up and walked out of the social worker's office and ducked into a nearby women's room. She couldn't breathe. This wasn't supposed to happen. Her talks with John Doe were private and now it seemed that everyone knew her secret. As much as she had prayed he would pull through this, she had to wonder now if she had crossed the line on this one. She got involved *personally* in this case. She had actually dared to care about the outcome. Could she get into trouble for this? Not again, she had made that mistake before and she paid for it. Surely she wouldn't get a second chance again if she screwed up mixing personal and professional lines. God, had she done something wrong? Mikey sat in the stall with her head in her hands. Think! She ordered herself.

Wait. Mikey shook her head. Was she just overreacting? Come on. All she did was console the victim of a tragic incident during her investigation. It wasn't wrong. It was *human.* Wasn't that what normal people did? People on the outside of the thick walls of the department.

The door to the bathroom opened and her body jolted. Someone had come in. She sat there motionless. She heard the soft squishy footsteps coming toward the stall.

"Mikey? Are you in there?"

The voice was familiar. It was Kim.

"Yes." She tried to keep her voice steady and light. She flushed the toilet to seem as if her visit to this room was more functional than escapism.

"Oh, well… I just spoke with Addison. She thought you seemed a little unsure about all this. Hey. I understand. You guys don't usually get involved in this end of the victim process. Hey. We all understand if you don't want to do this. And, I think it may be mostly my fault for making the connection. So, I really understand if you don't want to talk to the guy like some bad science experiment or something. It was just all we had to go on. Some of us have been working over our shifts to help out with him. That's why I am here so late."

Mikey forced herself up from the seat and closed her eyes. She struggled to find the plastic face she used when cases became hard to cope with. Yes, there it was. The cool, blank look that seemed void of any reaction but nonthreatening. She had it back.

Mikey exited the stall and smiled at Kim Lee. She walked to the sink and began to wash her hands.

"Well, I am not sure if I can help. But, whatever. Let's get this over with. It's been a long day and I really have things to do at home."

Mikey and the nurse walked the hall to an unfamiliar room. They walked in. It was less "medical" looking than the first one. This one had a night stand and TV and looked more like a patient's room than the one in the ICU.

They both stopped short of the bed and looked at the social worker who was waiting there.

"Hey, I think you have a visitor. It's Mikey."

The three of them looked at him as he laid there motionless in what appeared to be a deep sleep. No response.

"Hey, can you hear me? I said we brought someone to see you. It's Mikey." Addison looked up at the two women and raised her eyebrows in a questioning gesture.

"Maybe you should say something so he can hear you." Addison gestured for Mikey to come closer.

Mikey stiffly took one step and stopped. Her jaw was tense and she had completely developed the plastic face she needed for this moment. She was now searching for the plastic voice so she could open her mouth and speak.

"Yes, sir. I am Detective Michela Solitro from the Porto San Francesco Police Department. Sir, can you hear me?" The voice was forceful and monotone. It even sounded strange to even Mikey herself coming from her mouth.

No response from the dark-haired man lying in the bed before her.

Mikey looked at the social worker and shrugged her shoulders.

"Well, I guess I was wrong. It was the only thing I could think of. I am sorry about this. I mean, making you come down here so late." Kim Lee looked apologetically at Mikey. Her shoulders seemed to drop as she looked back at the man lying there.

Mikey looked at her and put her hand on her shoulder nodding.

"Thank you for trying." Addison smiled and walked out of the room.

"Yes, thank you. Well, we will just keep on trying with this one." Kim patted Mikey's hand and they walked out of the room together.

"No problem, Kim. I'm sorry for the reaction. You know. You guys do this stuff." Mikey began shaking her head again to clear it.

"No really, Mike. It's a lot to ask. These are tough cases. You do what you do… we do what we do. Thanks again, and I am sure I'll be seeing you soon."

"Sad but true. It never ends." Mikey agreed.

"Yea, I am going home. It has been a long day." Kim waved and walked to the nurses station to punch out for the night.

Mikey hesitated and looked at the door. She abruptly turned and walked to the stairs where she could make her escape and hopefully go home to repair the damage to her emotional walls.

The drive back to the house was flooded with images and emotions. There was no way Mikey was going to sleep. She took a quick turn and headed the car toward the pier. It would do her some good to think this through.

She sat in the dark on the edge of the pier staring out into the blackness of the bay. It seemed to match her mood. This night's events had scared her beyond imagination. Some of the fear came from self-preservation. She felt her face contort thinking about that. It was so *selfish*. Yes, that she was so worried about *herself* when there was this man lying there fighting for his opportunity to live. And, there was the flip side of her inner struggle. She was actually disappointed that he did not respond. Somewhere deep inside she wanted to be the reason this man lived. Maybe that was selfish too. She hadn't truly given it her best shot. Hell, she didn't even recognize her own voice in that room. Maybe that was all he was holding onto to get through this thing and she denied him that small comfort of familiarity with one voice that had truly cared about whether he lived or died. Wasn't it the idea that during a career if you had saved *one* person, then it was all worth it? Was he Mikey's one person?

Now Mikey had done it. She had created this moral and ethical mess inside her head. She laughed. Nothing was ever easy for her. She searched her soul for some direction. She had to know the truth. Surely everyone had left by now and the nurse on duty would let her back in. She could go back in private and answer the question that would plague her mind until she sought the answer.

Mikey almost ran to the car and retraced her path to the hospital. She practically ran up the stairs to the new floor and the unfamiliar nurses' station.

"Good evening."

The woman behind the desk looked at her and made an annoyed face before she quickly spoke...

"It is late, ma'am. Visiting hours are over. You will have to come back tomorrow."

"Yes, I know it is late. I was here a short while ago. I am from PSF PD. I had met with Kim Lee and Addison O'Neill. I would just like to see that patient for five minutes and will be out of your hair." Mikey leaned forward and gave the nurse behind the counter a reassuring smile while dropping the names of the staff.

"Oh, well... ok. I'm sorry. I am new to the floor. Sure... go ahead. It is..."

"Yes. I know. 14A. I was just here. Ha ha. Thank you. I'll be just a minute."

The nurse seemed reassured by her knowledge and smiled and went back to her work at the computer terminal.

Mikey walked silently to the room and hesitated before going inside. She almost didn't want to know the answer to the question she was attempting to answer. But, something pushed her inside. She went to the chair and sat down. She couldn't speak for a few minutes. She just watched him sleep. She summoned the nerve to speak.

"Hey. It's me, Mikey. I don't really know what to say tonight. I just want to say that I am sorry. I think I might have let you down earlier this evening. It wasn't the right thing to do. I asked you to hang in there and you did. That's great."

Mikey got up and moved to the bed. She reached out and took the hand that lay there motionless in the dimly lit room. She stood quietly for a minute when the hand reacted and closed grasping hers.

Mikey jumped and looked at the man. His eyes popped open and looked directly at her. They both were frozen and locked looking at each other. The man began to move his head and seemed to struggle a bit.

"Hey, it's okay. Don't move. It's okay." Mikey saw the effort the man was making and he looked uncomfortable.

His mouth opened and a scratchy sound started to come out. She couldn't make it out at first. She leaned forward closer. It began again and her face softened at the words…

"I see… *you* now, Mikey."

Mikey stood frozen locked meeting the eyes of a stranger that seemed so familiar.

"You *heard* me? All those nights I talked to you. You actually heard me?"

"Yes." The voice managed to squeek out the word.

Her hand reached out to touch his cheek without thinking, without calculating the response or even the consequence of the simple motion. And for several minutes, Mikey was truly calm and at peace looking at the man in amazement.

It didn't last and Mikey knew she had to tell her new friend something urgent.

"Okay. Look. I need you to understand something I have to tell you. It is very important. I really bent some rules by coming to the hospital to see you every night. I could get into a lot of trouble and lose my job. And, what is worse, I would not be allowed to see you anymore. So, we have to make a deal. I will promise to come by as often as I can. But, you cannot tell on me to the staff here. Okay?"

Mikey looked into the eyes that had not moved from her face. She waited and thought that maybe he didn't understand until she felt his hand squeeze hers and he managed a slight nod in the affirmative. She knew the nurse would wonder what she was doing and come checking soon.

"Ok, I see you didn't let me down. And, I will keep my promise to you as long as I don't get caught. So, I have to go. I'll be back tomorrow night. You get focused on getting stronger. On just getting better. Do you hear me?"

"Yes." The man managed to scratch the sound from his mouth.

"Okay. You keep working on getting better and we can talk more. It will give me a reason to open your case if you can talk and remember things to help me. So, the number one goal right now is for you to recover. You work on that, okay?"

The man made a feeble nod.

"Okay. Good night. I will see you tomorrow. Sleep well."

Mikey lingered for a second not wanting to let go of his hand. She gave it a squeeze and quickly left the room. She managed a smile for the nurse at the station.

"Oh, was he awake?"

"No, he just slept." Mikey smiled and the nurse waved at her as she passed by.

Mikey drove home wondering what had just happened. And, how would she be able to visit John Doe each night without causing suspicion or anyone asking questions. Or even worse, John Doe maybe telling them that she was indeed 'Mikey.' She clenched her eyes shut for a minute. Too late to worry about some of that. So, the next best thing was to control what was ahead. It was scary, but something about it felt really... *good.* She made it home and climbed into bed with her small glass of spirits. She enjoyed the warm sensation it caused and eased the racing of her mind. She would have liked to stay awake for hours contemplating this new situation, but it was a school night and the alarm would sound early. She drifted off to sleep and hoped that tomorrow would unlock some of the mystery she encountered today.

Over the following weeks, Mikey had managed to create a routine. She was able to visit with John Doe three to five nights a week depending on her work load. The best part was going to see Kim and Addison and manage to smooth over her first surprise visit. She asked if she could still visit John Doe in the hopes of being there if he developed the ability to speak and remember the events that transpired in the tunnel on the night he was injured. They both thought it was a good idea since no one visited him and she would be his only contact aside from hospital staff.

John's recovery had been "a miracle" as Dr. Kauffman put it. He was now able to sit up and talk. His speech and motor skills were still sluggish, but his eyes were sharp and clear. He seemed to comprehend his surroundings well and had been starting to ask questions. The only problem was that he had no memory from before the hospital. This left Mikey with the same problems. Who was he and what happened to him? She talked to him and encouraged him to remember regularly but he seemed to grow tired easily so she never pressed him too hard. He had only been *awake* for several months now. His curiosity was increasing. John Doe asked so many questions. It was like he was experiencing life for the first time. Dr. Kauffman thought that this could be normal because of his memory loss and because of his previous disability that seemed to have been "cured" by the whole incident. Mikey began nodding her head as she was driving. He was truly a miracle and she looked forward to each day when she could spend time with him. He was so refreshing to her tired mind. Mikey was so lost in her thoughts that she almost didn't hear her cell phone ring.

"Hello?"

"Mikey. Hey, it's Addison from the hospital."

"Hi Addie. What's up?"

"Well, I just wanted to let you know the latest on our friend, John. The doctor was in to see him today. He feels that John needs more physical therapy than we can offer him right now. He made some calls and got a center about fifty miles away to take him for the next leg of his recovery. Isn't that GREAT! I didn't think anyone would accept him since he was indigent, but the doc called in a favor. He really thinks that there is a possibility that John can fully recover if he had an in-house placement. I was so excited. I just had to call and tell you."

Mikey was silent for a moment while she composed herself to speak.

"Mikey?"

"Yea, sorry. I am driving. Ha. Yea, that is great. So, when are they sending him?"

"That is the best part. Probably tomorrow morning. They are willing to get going right away. He is everyone's favorite pet project since no one has seen anything like this."

"Wow. Um, that is so great. How long will he be up there?"

"Well, I am not sure, Mikey. I guess that depends on him and how he does. It is not my area. But, I have had patients go for maybe four to twelve weeks. Something like that. He is a special case, so again, I am not sure."

"Oh, I see. After that, what will happen to him?"

"Well, I think that we will have to keep working on that. I have a case open here for him and I can try to see what is out there as far as assistance – housing, social programs, re-education programs… The whole thing. So, I will work with the rehab center's social worker. He may come back here or we may find another location for him that serves his needs the best. Then I guess we will get him into the state system once we see how he does. Again, I am not sure."

"Oh, well… Ok. Thanks for calling me. I guess I can still work on who he is while he is up there. I will go by again tonight and wish him well. Thanks again."

"You are welcome, Mikey. Have a great day."

Mikey frowned. She hadn't considered that they would send John Doe away. What if he remembered something and wasn't here to tell her about it? What was more was there would be a huge hole in her life now. She hadn't thought about much of anything outside of work and seeing John Doe. This may be good for him, but this was certainly going to be bad for her. She felt a wistful pain of loss and she began to fight back tears. It served her right for getting involved in this mess.

Mikey made it through the remainder of the work day and put on her plastic face for her visit at the hospital. It was early and there would still be staff so that she and John Doe could not converse as freely as she had come to enjoy. But, she managed to get to the hospital and talk with him for a while. Mikey tried not to look directly at him fearing that he may see the sadness she was feeling. She tried to be upbeat and encourage him to do his best at the new facility. She noticed that he did not look at her much either. She explained that he could let the new staff know if he remembered anything and to contact her directly. She gave him her card. She left another to be given with his records for the new staff. It was the best she could do for now. She went to his bedside and squeezed his hand. He squeezed hers in return. The silent exchange lasted seconds, but left Mikey feeling confused and feeling at a loss for what to say or do next. She looked at him and he smiled at her. She couldn't smile back.

"I hope I see you again, John Doe. Good luck." Mikey released his hand and turned and left the hospital. It would be a long night. She was surely going to be a wreck trying to sort this whole thing out. Why did this have to happen? Ah, she thought. It was starting already.

9

"*H* ello?"
       "Hello. Dot?"
"Helloooo?"
Hello! Dot, what's up?
"Who is calling?"
Mikey exhaled. Here were the theatrics she had wanted
to avoid.
"Dot. It's Mikey."
"Who?"
"Dorthea. It is Michela. I just called to say hi. I know I
haven't called for a while. I'm sorry. I just had a lot going
on. So, what is up?"
"A while? Mikey... it has been three months and not a
word. You didn't return my calls."
"Yea, I... I... well I know. Dot, things were just a little
complicated. It's hard to explain right now. But, I really
have missed you."
"What? No one else to turn to?"

"Dot, don't be mean. I said I was sorry, okay?" Mikey sighed loudly into the phone.

"Whatever Mikey."

Mikey sat silently with the phone against her ear. She had been crying and just wished someone could understand her right now. It was possible that even Dorthea wasn't going to listen.

"Mike? Are you there?"

"Yea."

"Alright, alright. What is it?"

"I was just hoping that we could go out for a drink or something. I have got to get out of the house for a while. Can you go?"

"What? Right now? God Mikey. You don't talk to me for months and then just drop in out of the blue. You are impossible."

"Well, yea, I guess so." Mikey hadn't considered that her friend could be busy. She had forgotten that other people had *lives* that were more complicated than her own.

"If you can't go, Dot, it's alright."

"No, no. Don't be silly. Sure, where do you want to go? I know something's up."

"O'Malley's okay?"

"Sure Mike. I'll be there in forty-five minutes. See you there."

"Okay."

Mikey and Dorthea sat at a small table in the dimly lit bar and grill. Without much prodding, Mikey began to tell Dorthea the whole story. She started at the beginning and continued to the very end without interruption. Mikey finally looked up at her friend. She wasn't quite able to read the expression on Dorthea's face. Maybe she shouldn't have told her. The silence was getting uncomfortable and she had to look away.

"What are you thinking, Dot? I tell you the whole story and you just sit there."

"I am thinking. The first thing that comes to my mind is wow. This is not you at all Mike. Not at all. I can't believe that you could get so caught up in this guy. It's so out of character for you. You know, you're such a hermit! And, you above all people hanging out with someone you really don't *know*. What if he is crazy or a serial killer or something. Mikey! You don't even know who he is!"

"Dot, he's not a killer. Stop it."

"Mikey, for goodness sake. You really don't *know* that. Girl, really. You have got to get a LIFE! I mean, hang out with the living. No, instead you find some kind of bond with a person you don't know and who isn't really able to do anything. It is like you selected a dead body to hang out with. I don't know about you, Mikey. I think either they are putting something in the water down at the PD or you are just losing it. Either way I think it is best you just let go of Mr. Nobody and start getting out and doing things. All this isolation is making you nuts. You did a good deed. That's all. Now dust yourself off and forget about it."

Mikey sat there quietly while Dot went on and on. She really didn't understand at all. Well, in all fairness, who would? Worst of all, what if Dot was right? Maybe she was really losing it. Mikey began shaking her head while Dot continued to talk about some friend of a friend and how she could arrange for her to meet him. Here we go again. Mikey rolled her eyes. Maybe calling Dot was a mistake. Mikey wondered if she could take the extremes. She went from spending time with someone who spoke very little to

Dot who could not seem to shut up. Mikey took advantage of this time to finally sip her drink and hope that it might at least drown out some of Dots ideas.

Mikey and her friend finally finished their evening and were walking to the parking lot. Dorthea had still not stopped listing an endless supply of people and events she was planning for Mikey. Mikey was definitely ready to go home. She feared she had wasted her evening and could have at least stayed home to cry it out. God, what could she do *without* John Doe and *with* all these scenarios of torture being painted by Dorthea? Wait. That was it. What had Dorthea said? Mikey had been spending all her time with someone she didn't know. Yes. That was it. THAT was what she was going to do while he was gone. Mikey was going to fill her time finding out who he was. She had spent time on it in the beginning, but then spent the extra time with John Doe himself. This would be a great time to really ramp up the energy on that part of the investigation. He may be gone, but she would still be working on the case and keeping the promise she made not to give up. She began smiling walking next to Dorthea.

"Mike? Are you listening? Why are you smiling like that? You just tell me you are depressed and sad and now you are smiling like a Cheshire cat. Are you up to something or are you just crazy?"

"Just crazy Dot. Just crazy." Mikey continued to smile until they parted in the lot and went in their separate directions. She started to plan her course on this case. She had six to twelve weeks to figure out who was John Doe. At least it was something to fill the void.

Mikey showed up at work early. She had so much to do. Mikey had filled a full notebook page by the time Detective Harris entered the office.

"Good morning."

"Good morning, John."

"You get here early or what?" The detective looked at the stack of shuffled papers across Mikey's desk.

"Yea, a little. Just catching up a little. You look like you had a rough night."

"Ha, yea. We had company in from out of town. They stayed late. So, what are we behind on?"

"Oh, nothing, just my parts… you know. Notes and stuff."

"Oh, well okay. Hey, I gotta run up to the hospital first thing today. The records are in on that last abuse case. Faster to pick them up than wait on them to come in the mail. So, I'll see you after roll call."

"Okay, see ya." Mikey didn't look up as she was already working on the second page of notes for the Doe case. Mikey finally stopped and thought that this should just about do it. And, it might take three months to complete as she reviewed the list. She would have to get this done after her new cases. She would be busy.

Mikey went immediately to the dispatch floor. She needed to do this first thing. Maybe her search had been too small. Maybe that is why John Doe's missing report didn't turn up. She would ask the operator to do a wider sweep that maybe included several states. Surely that would be big enough.

"Hi Cathy."

"Hi Detective Solitro. How are you this morning?"

"Good, thanks. And you?"

"Okay. What can I do for you?"

"Well, I had you enter information on a John Doe months back. And you did a missing person query for me. Well, I never did get a hit or anything close on it. I was wondering if you could expand that for me?"

"Oh, yea. I remember that one. They reopened that case? Wow. I thought that one was toast. Well, okay. How much wider are you wanting to go?"

"Uh… well… all adjacent states."

"Damn! Now that is going to take a little time. You don't need this right now do you?"

"No, no. When you can get to it. That's all. I'd be happy if you could get it in about a week. That sound okay?"

"Well, yea. I could do it then in between the other entries. Yea. That is do-able."

"Okay Cathy. Thanks. Just call me when you get it done."

Mikey hurried back to the unit to get to roll call on time. It seemed to take forever to get her assignments and get back to the office. She raced through the cases and left notes on the pile for Harris. Mikey was anxious to get on the street. She was sure there was still something out there that might lead to John Doe. The case was cold, but it was still possible. She made her way to the unmarked cruiser and was off toward the pier. It was late morning and the boats would have left early in the morning. But, luckily it looked like a storm coming and maybe some of the fishermen would have returned early. She may run into a few more of them that she hadn't spoken with already.

Mikey parked and hurried to the pier. There were still several boats tied up and the crew working to beat the weather. She would just go one by one.

"Morning!" Mikey smiled at the man working on the pier.

"Morning ma'am."

"Sir, I am Detective Solitro from PSF PD. I am conducting an investigation on an unidentified man found around the 4th of July. Do you have a minute?"

"Sure."

Mikey gave a brief synopsis of the incident and the description of the man to now include the additional knowledge that he may have been handicapped. The sailor didn't recollect seeing him and summoned his crew to the pier. He relayed the information and one by one, they all denied seeing anyone who fit the description. Mikey left him with a card in case he should remember anything and made her way to the next boat.

"Hello, sir."

The man standing on the deck of the boat eyed her cautiously.

"I am Detective Solitro from PSF PD. Can I talk to you a minute?"

The man stood there for a moment and shook his head.

"Do you have a warrant?"

Mikey was startled by the remark for a moment.

"No no no. I am not from the Port Authority. Sir, I am just investigating an unidentified person. I don't know what is on your boat or supposed to be on your boat. Nor, do I care. I just want to ask you and your crew about a particular man from around the 4th of July. That is it."

"I don't think so. Come back when you have a warrant." The man turned his back and walked to the other end of the boat.

He was *nice* Mikey thought. There was one more boat. Mikey began to walk toward it when she saw some kind of commotion on the pier where it had docked. Some loud noise… yelling. It was still a ways away but she could see the figure of someone that appeared to be… dancing or something. She hesitated after the last exchange and wondered what was going on down there. She paused for a few seconds and remembered John Doe. Mikey marched forward determined to ask anyone she could find. No matter how crazy or dangerous it seemed.

The closer Mikey got to the last boat docked, she could see the crew scurrying around on deck and on the pier removing their catch and cleaning the vessel before the storm came in. The figure on the pier that seemed to be the source of the noise was not drawing the attention of any of the crew. She was perplexed but kept moving forward. She would find out soon enough.

Mikey arrived at the boat. She quickly noted the source of the commotion to be an older gentleman who was marching and shouting out some cadence mixed with orders and some military jargon. Strange. Mikey walked up to the boat and the man closest to it.

"Hello, sir. I am Detective Solitro. Can I talk to you for a moment?"

The man quickly snapped upright and then looked at the man making all the noise.

"Detective, uh. I am so sorry. He does this all the time. We will try to keep his volume down. 'General! General, Sir! We have a complaint from HQ about the noise. They said we have to keep it down or risk the enemy finding our location."

The man marching around in a circle near the boat stopped on a dime and looked at the fisherman.

"Roger that, sailor." He quietly kept marching but without the noise part.

"There. See ma'am. We'll keep him quiet. We are not trying to disturb anyone."

"Well, sir. That is not the reason I am here, but now you have me curious. Is he one of your *crew*?"

"Aw, no ma'am. He lives here somewhere. He is a little… well, not to be harsh or anything. He is a little off. He saw a lot in the Vietnam war. He is an old man and he comes here and meets us every day. We like him. I don't know how he supports himself or anything and we give him some food each day. That's all."

"What's his name?"

"To be honest, I don't know. He calls himself the General. That's what we call him."

"Huh. Well, actually I am looking for someone that may be a little like him. Could I have a minute?"

"Sure. What can I do for you?"

"Well, I have a case. It involves a man that was injured and unidentified back around July 4th. He may have been disabled. He is about six feet tall, thin, light complexion, longer brown hair and brown eyes. Have you or any of your crew had any sightings of this guy?"

"Let me ask." The man walked aboard and called the crew to the desk. He conveyed the description and all shook their heads in the negative.

"I'm sorry ma'am, but no one here remembers seeing anyone like that. We aren't docked long. Just long enough to remove the catch and clean the boat. And, feed the General. That's it."

"Oh, well okay. I was hoping someone had seen him. I'll leave you my card and if you or your crew remember anything, would you please call me?"

"Sure." The man reached out and took the card.

"Have a good day, sir."

"You too."

"That sounds like the wounded soldier. Are you from head quarters?"

"Excuse me?" Mikey turned to look at the man they called the General.

"Yes, I think I saw him. We found him underground. I think the enemy had been torturing him. Me and Annie rescued him and took him back to our camp. He was doing okay there for a while. Annie is the nurse for our post. Well, he must have been important because the enemy planned a strike and while he was out with Annie to see the medics. They recaptured him!"

Mikey looked blankly at the man in front of her. She then turned to look at the fisherman with questioning eyes. He shrugged his shoulders.

"I see… General. Wow. Okay. I'll have to add that to my report. Thank you for your information. You have been a great help." Mikey discreetly winked at the fisherman who smiled in return.

"You are welcome. It was a great hardship to lose one like that. It completely destroyed the nurse. War is hell you know."

"I have been told that sir. Thank you for your service."

"It was my duty, ma'am. I hope you find the soldier. Can I get one of those cards in case we see him again?"

"Thank you and yes. By all means. Here you go. Good day gentlemen."

The fisherman gave her a wave and the General saluted as she turned and walked away. Too bad the only news about John Doe came from a crazy old man living forty or more years in the past. Great. Well it was getting late and she had to return to the office for more interviews on the new cases. The next step on the list would have to wait until later or tomorrow.

Mikey looked up at the clock upon entering the office. She still had five minutes to spare. Detective Harris was at his desk writing when she walked in.

"Hey. I am back. How'd it go at the hospital?"

Harris looked up and seemed annoyed. Wow. Had he been that consumed in his writing that she ticked him off by interrupting?

"What?" She asked him.

"What the hell have you been doing up there at the hospital?" He glared now at her.

"What?"

"You know what! I go up there to get some papers and run into Kim. Oh she goes on and on about the guy from the subway and how you have been there every step of the way. Mikey. The LT closed that case months ago. So what were you *doing* up there?"

"Nothing. Well, just hanging around in case he remembered anything. I mean. We knew at first that he was in a coma and he couldn't talk yada yada yada. Well, he came around. Woke up, you know and he started to talk a little and I was hoping that he would remember something. We never did *ID* the guy John."

"I don't care. Since when did you get promoted and reopen cases? What were you thinking? Mikey. Do you have a death wish or something?"

"No! I am just saying that we shouldn't have left it hanging wide open like that. If I have time I continue to check on the case. What if something turns up and we are looking the other way. I am not behind in anything else. I am just keeping the door open a crack in case something comes our way. That's all."

"Well, from the story I got from the hospital, it sounds like the door is not cracked but wide open. I am telling you Mike. Leave that shit alone. It seems like you might be getting a little too close to that case to be objective. So drop it."

"John. I can't just drop it. It seems so wrong. I promise I won't do anything stupid or crazy. I am just keeping my finger on it. Hell, the guy isn't even here anymore. They sent him somewhere for additional treatment or something. I am just running little leads if and when they turn up. If something comes that is major, I'll go to the LT and ask to reopen it. That's all."

"It sounds like you never actually closed it to me. Gee, how did it go? Oh yea. 'Ok Harris, we can't waste time on every bleeding heart case that goes unsolved. We would have mountains on our desks.' Remember those words? They were yours when I first came to the unit. So, what gives Mike?"

"John. I think you are overreacting. Nothing. Sue me. I just think that there is a possibility that I can figure it out. That's all."

"Yea, you can figure yourself on a good suspension if you get caught. So, leave me out of it. I think it is your ego. You couldn't pull this one together solo so you just can't let it go."

"You know? I don't care what you think. How about that. Just don't go ratting me out like a little girl."

"I am not saying a word Mike. But I am not lying for you either. So, sink or swim on your own. I don't want to talk about the damned case again. The less I know about it, the better off I am." The large man pounded his hand onto the desk and the sound was loud enough to gain the attention of everyone three offices away.

"Good." Mikey scowled at his lack of faith in her. She rolled her eyes. Like she would get *him* in trouble. Yea, the old story that kept coming back. Like the trouble she got O'Rourke into. Mikey rolled her eyes again just thinking the words. Would it ever die?

"Good. You are an idiot Mike."

"Whatever. What did you get from the hospital? Can we start there again? Or do you want to attract more attention and beat on the desk some more?"

Detective Harris shoved the documents at her and continued writing his report.

The day seemed to drag on in the unusual quiet of the office absent any conversation. She counted the seconds until she could finish up and just get out of there. It was late and there wasn't time to re-comb all the neighborhoods between the pier and the subway station. She decided to just drive and see if anyplace was open to just do one thing tonight. She kept driving and saw the lights to one business that seemed to still be operating. She pulled over and got out and walked to the store front.

It was a nice place. Mikey had never really been in here before. She would have to check her list to see if she had canvassed the store months ago. An older man appeared out of the back room and came quickly to the counter.

"Yes? I am sorry. We were just closing and I got detained in the back. I might be able to get you something but most of our hot dishes and meats have been put away for the evening."

"Oh, I see. I am sorry to disturb you. Uh, I am Detective Solitro from the police department. I have been working on a case from back in July. I know it has been some time ago. I just keep hoping I am going to find someone that has seen a person that remains unidentified. Do you have a minute?"

"Sure."

"First, sir, if you don't mind, what is your name? It is just so I know who I have spoken with and don't keep coming back here to bother you. That's all."

"Sure. It is Jacob Berwitz."

"Well, Mr. Berwitz. I am looking for anyone who may have seen a man around that time." Mikey went on to explain and describe the man to the kind merchant who waited patiently until she finished.

"No, I can't say that I saw him. We have so many people that pass through. Well, I suppose you already know that. And, you just never know with them. We had a woman we helped here for more than a year. Then, she just one day showed up like she lost her best friend. She was quite hysterical and then disappeared and we have no idea what became of her. My poor wife worried herself sick over it. It was around that time. We liked her so much. We just never saw her again after that. Those people are unpredictable and they often appear and disappear without any notice. It is sad. We really miss her sometimes. She was a big help. Maybe we should have reported her missing? Do you think? She seemed different than the rest of them."

"Uh, well, I don't know. I would advise if you think there was some type of foul play then yes. If not, she was free to leave whenever she wanted."

"Yes, I guess you are right. I have learned my lesson with all of that. No more. And, I am sorry I couldn't help you. I hope you find the poor soul."

"Thank you Mr. Berwitz. Please take my card. I just don't want to give up. So, if you remember anything, please call me. Any detail is important. Even if it seems small." The detective nodded.

"Yes. I sure will. Please be safe officer."

Mikey smiled. This was a nice man.

"I will sir. Thank you." Mikey shook the man's hand and left the deli. Didn't *anyone* see him before this happened? How the hell does an entire city miss… miss what? One man? Mikey shook her head and went back to her car. It was like finding a needle in a haystack. She couldn't talk to each and every of the city's 120,000 inhabitants. And… even if she did, there was no guarantee that if someone knew something that they would even *tell* her. Damn it. Maybe Harris was right. She decided that this was enough for today. Mikey walked to her car and drove home. She tried not to think. She walked in and washed up and ran to the bedroom. She turned on the music and poured her favorite anesthesia. The liquor would taste good tonight since she felt the whole day had left a bad taste in her mouth. She laid back onto the pillows and sipped her nightly poison. She allowed her mind to ponder the impossibility of identifying John Doe. It was so big. She laughed and decided she would accept that he had been deposited by aliens and call it a night. Maybe they had room in their spaceship for one more… then from sheer exhaustion, her mind turned off.

10

"Good morning, Mikey. How's it going today?" Detective Harris walked to his desk and waited for his partner's response.

"Mike?" The man looked at Mikey who seemed to be in a trance looking out of the window.

"What?" Mikey jerked around to look at him.

"Didn't you hear me?"

"Um, no. I'm sorry. What?"

"*I said good morning.*"

"Oh, yea. Good morning John." Mikey started shuffling the pile of papers on her desk and situated herself to begin the day.

"Mike. What is up with you? Are you *still* mad at me over the subway case or what? You haven't really said ten words to me… no, to anyone for months. You want to talk about it?"

Mikey nervously looked away knowing that she had not been herself. Whatever that was. She felt her face tense and forced a response.

"No, I am fine. Really. I guess I am just a little burned out. That's all." Mikey forced a little smile and went back to the paperwork in front of her.

"Well, at least Christmas is just around the corner. That should give us a little break. The crap seems to slow down and we get a few days off. Do you have any plans?"

Mikey started to feel annoyed. Her teeth clenched. What was with the twenty questions?

"Uh, no. Not yet. I like to play it by ear. You?" That was the key. Now he would start talking about family parties and presents and she could pretend to be listening without having to answer any more questions. She just kept nodding her head while he talked. The lieutenant's door swung open and banged against the filing cabinet. Both detectives jumped.

"Solitro. Get in here."

Wide-eyed, Mikey got up and made her way to the open office door and slipped inside and up to the big desk.

"Yes LT?" Mikey stood motionless wondering what she could have done to bring this on.

"Do you realize that when I check the vacation totals that you have not taken one of your days off since March? That leaves you with 17 days of vacation on the books. What? Were you planning on giving it back? Jesus. You *lose* the vacation time if you don't use it. And that will be just great. The union reps will be filing grievances and the captain will be giving me shit. When were you planning on taking this time off?"

Mikey stood there suddenly sheepish. How could she have forgotten about it? It just slipped her mind. She did the same thing each day like a robot and there were no plans to jog her memory. She just looked at the older man behind the desk and shrugged her shoulders.

"That's great. Well, I will tell you what. I am going to schedule it for you. Work out the week and take off until the 28th. That will clear up the vacation balance. You totally screwed up my staffing schedule. I don't want this to happen again. I had already approved vacation for this month and now I have to go back over it all. Don't let this happen again." He grunted and nodded toward the door.

Mikey quickly exited the office and returned to her desk a little shocked.

"What happened?" Harris was looking at the lieutianant's door and then back at Mikey.

"Oh, well. I guess I forgot to turn in my vacation schedule. Seems that I have three weeks left and now I messed up the unit staffing during the holidays. Yea, he's mad."

"Geez, Mike. You could have gave the time to me! Really? Who forgets to take their vacation? You are crazy. Well, there's the break you said you needed." Harris turned back to his desk relieved that this had nothing to do with their joint work. He hated the wrath of the lieutenant. He chuckled and started looking over the papers on his desk.

Mikey sat numbly at her desk. What would she do with herself for three weeks if she didn't have to go to work? That was a long time to sit in the house waiting for it to be over. Why couldn't she just lose the time? It was better than taking it off. At least for her. What a perfect present for Christmas. A prison sentence of house arrest for three weeks. Great. Mikey started to think about what she could possibly do with that time. Certainly she could see Dorthea one night. Ok, that left 20 more days to occupy. She would have to go past the bookstore Friday and get ten books. Maybe she could escape in them until the time ended. She didn't have a better plan than that. It would have to do.

The next several days seemed to fly by while Mikey was working at two hundred percent getting all her cases together before her sentenced time off. Each file was up-to-date including case notes and a cover sheet of any further work to be done. It should be easy for John to figure out if any of them broke while she was off. Or, if the LT came demanding the status. Good. She didn't want to punish John for her oversight. So, that was it. She was finished here and in ten minutes, the banishment would begin. She grabbed the note she had made of a list of books. She would hit the book store first and then the state store for a supply of Black Velvet. She would be stocked for the duration.

Mikey finally arrived at home after spending hours selecting books that just might hold her interest for the next several weeks. She took the big bag along with the other one clanging with bottles into the bedroom and sat them on the bed. She figured she would shower and get started with book one tonight. It was something to do. She hoped it would be good. The clerk helped her pick them out. Mikey took her time and enjoyed the hot water and the smell of the soap. There was no reason to rush tonight. She had nowhere to go tomorrow. She finished and dried off and slid into a set of warm cotton pajamas. Now she was ready to begin her escape in the first book.

Mikey snuggled under the covers and carefully propped the book up on a pillow on her stomach and sat the glass containing her nightly spirit on the night stand. She was ready. Chapter one… Mikey began reading. The first few pages were slow. It was possibly because she really didn't want to read. But, the opportunity to escape was a greater motivation. She kept reading and sipping hoping the book would become her ticket to somewhere else.

Mikey was going along until the sixth chapter. She had smelled it coming but kept hoping the story would take a different turn.

"NO WAY!" Mikey yelled as she flipped and scanned the next several pages. Mikey mumbled out loud... "I *told* the clerk. *No romances.* I hate them." Mikey slammed the book shut and sat there stewing. She hated these kinds of books. They were so... so... unrealistic. These stories didn't happen in real life. They were just a waste of time. They made people want what didn't exist. Real romance. There was no such thing. Great. Mikey tossed the book across the bed. Now what? Mikey rolled her eyes and sat there in the dimly lit, silent room. She just laid there and sipped her potion. Tomorrow was another day. She would try a different book.

Mikey stared at the sofa and then scanned the rest of the room. She had managed to rearrange the furniture in three rooms, twice each. It had been four days. That was it. Four days. At least she had managed to find one book about aliens that seemed to be doing the trick. She was almost finished. She had left several messages for Dorthea today, but still no return call. Mikey was hoping she would call today. She was feeling a little claustrophobic and there was nowhere else to move the furniture. Maybe she could paint the bathroom? She was thinking about a color scheme when the phone rang. Fantastic! It would be Dorthea.

"Hello?"

"Yes, may I speak to Detective Solitro?"

Mikey paused. This was not Dorthea. And, she was on *vacation*. She thought about saying it was a wrong number or just hanging up. She hesitated. Wait. Maybe this was the break she was looking for. Something has happened in one of her cases. She would *have* to go back to work. The voice on the other end repeated the request.

"Yes, yes. This is she." Mikey was anxious to hear the details.

"Yes, I am sorry to bother you. I tried your office number first and they advised me you were on vacation. I tried back again today and they said you would be off for a few weeks. So, I hated to call your personal number, but it *was* in the file."

"Oh no problem. No problem at all. What can I do for you?" Mikey had already grabbed a pen and paper for the details.

"Good, I am Stella Goodrich. I am the social worker at Mercy Arms."

"Uh huh." Mikey was scribbling down the information waiting for the woman to continue.

"Well, our patient is ready to be released. He has requested to go back to PSF Hospital to finish his recovery. He insisted that we notify you of his return."

"Who?" Mikey was confused.

"Oh, I'm sorry. I am a little ahead of myself. The patient was sent here from your area hospital. We are up north. The patient is only known as John Doe. There were several places that he had to choose from to continue his recovery. Several were probably better suited to his needs, but he has insisted to return to PSF. He is doing so well the doctors here allowed his request to return. So, we normally notify the family contact. That was blank in his file and he requested that you be notified of his return."

Mikey stood motionless and silent comprehending the message she was receiving. She couldn't even blink. Her throat was tight and her mind had stalled.

"Hello? Are you still there?"

"Yes. I am. Yes."

"Is there a problem, ma'am?"

"No, no. There is no problem." Mikey's mind began to churn again and she clenched her eyes shut to focus.

"*When* is he scheduled to return?"

"Well, it has been set up for days now. He will be returned to the hospital there tomorrow morning. Probably around eleven o'clock – a.m."

"I see. Okay. That's great. Thank you very much. Is there anything else?"

"No ma'am. That is it."

"Ok, thanks again for letting me know. Goodbye."

Mikey quickly hung up and stood in the center of the room in shock. It was *him* again. He was coming back. She had forced him out of her mind for these past months. Wait. What did the woman say? *He* had asked them to call her. He must be doing better. And, he wanted her to know he was back. Oh wait...

Mikey walked over the newly positioned sofa and sat down. What was she thinking? They probably had to call somebody, right? So, she would be the only non-medical person listed. Whatever. But, then... now what? Was she *expected* to go to the hospital? *Should* she go? Oh good grief. Mikey felt herself becoming agitated and confused. She reminded herself of what Harris told her. This case was closed. Period. Crap. What if PSF Hospital just called her again when he arrived? Maybe it would be best to go and then have her name removed from the file. Surely the staff here knew her well enough that if something came up that she needed to know, they would call. She could talk to Addison about it and get that whole social worker thing set up for him and that would be it. Yes, that would probably be the best thing to do. Get this straightened out. She was off tomorrow and could be there promptly at eleven. She wondered what the hell she could do now to occupy herself until eleven a.m. tomorrow? It was going to be a long day.

Mikey arrived at the hospital just before eleven. She looked at herself in the rearview mirror. She looked tired. But, then again, not too bad for not having slept for one minute last night. She couldn't understand why she felt so nervous. She told herself that she was being ridiculous and that Harris and Dorthea had good reason to have her committed. She had no idea where they would be taking him. She decided to start with Addison's office and get that part out of the way first.

Mikey walked the busy hallway to the social worker's office. The clerk advised her that Ms. O'Neill would be out to see her shortly. She had a seat in the waiting area. She was greatful for the opportunity to compose herself, but she still felt like coming out of her skin. Maybe too much coffee? She nervously tapped her foot.

"Detective?"

"Yes?"

"Ms. O'Neill can see you now. Go right in."

"Thank you." Mikey got up and quickly walked to the inner office and entered.

"Good morning, Detective. How are you?"

"Good morning. I am good. How about you?" Mikey felt a little shaky and sat in a chair close to the door before being asked to sit.

"Great. Thank you. Well I suppose I know why you are here. They told me that they had called you for the notification. The plans had to be changed to accommodate an emergency placement for early this morning. So, they actually brought him in last night. He got here just before midnight. They would have called you but it was so late that it didn't seem appropriate. I wasn't sure if you would be able to make it this morning with your work schedule, so we decided to get him settled and go from there."

Mikey started to fidget in the seat.

"He's already here?"

"Yes, like I said, since last night. I must say he has caused quite a stir already. The nurses are already crazy about him. This place can be so ridiculous. But even *I* couldn't believe it *myself*. He has just done *so well!* He is truly a miracle. Nurse Lee has been wanting to call you all morning, but I didn't want to… well bother you too much about all of this. I mean, this part is usually done with *family* and it is such an unusual situation. So, I will leave the rest up to you."

"The rest of what?" Mikey was now leaning forward in her chair to understand fully.

"Well, Mr. *Doe* has selected Central House to continue his recovery. That is right here in the Central District. It wouldn't have been my first choice. But, I won't fight it. The place has a decent reputation. He should be placed there in about a week. There is just some preparation for the move and to designate a mentor for his transitional period. We'll talk about that more later. Do you want to see him?"

Mikey's mind was swirling with questions. Transition? Mentor? She was overwhelmed. John Doe was nearly vegetative when he left here. Where were they putting him? Surely they weren't going to dump him into some nursing home to just rot away there. Her mind was racing and she was again nervously tapping her foot.

"Yes, I would like to see him." Mikey had decided that she would see what shape John Doe was in before she released him to the outside world. She was already getting angry that he may just be dumped off like some kind of refuse. She followed alongside the social worker to a part of the hospital that was unfamiliar. It seemed to take forever to get there. She didn't speak a word fearing that she would vent on this poor woman who had done so much for John Doe. Mikey assumed there were limits to what the hospital could do. How much was all of this costing them? She didn't want to even think about it. She would just see how he was and try to be satisfied with whatever placement they could make for him. She remained quiet until they reached the end of a long hall and turned right.

"This is it." Ms. O'Neill pointed into the room. It looked more like a suite than a hospital room. There was a bed but it was accompanied by furniture. There was a table and chairs and a sofa and TV. There were people sitting in the seats talking. She briefly glanced at them and saw they were wearing hospital uniforms. She focused on the neatly made bed and stopped. The bed was empty. Didn't she say he was already here? She stood puzzled for a moment and thought that maybe they had taken him for tests and that she should find a seat with the staff until he returned.

Mikey quickly found a vacant chair at the table and sat down. She pulled out her notebook and prepared a page in case she would need it for notes later. She had secret notes that she kept on this case hidden in the back of her desk.

Mikey heard movement and looked up. A younger nurse was standing up and looking at her smiling.

"Okay, I have to go." She seemed to be making an announcement.

Mikey returned to the paper in front of her and heard the others saying something about getting back to work. God, what was this, the lunch room? Mikey shook her head and continued to write.

The sound of someone clearing their throat got Mikey's attention. She looked up at the man standing in front of her.

"Yes?" She looked at his hospital attire but there was no name tag.

"Hi Mikey." The man stood there smiling.

"Hi." Mikey nodded at him and then her eyes narrowed looking at the man.

"Is that... *you?*" Mikey's mouth began to fall open as she looked over the man in front of her.

"*Wait?* Is that really you?" Mikey stood up from her seat looking at...

"Yes. It's me." The man began smiling and nodding his head.

Mikey stood up and took several steps backward to assess the man. This was impossible. But, she could see the similarity in the features of the man that she spent so many evenings with just sharing her thoughts. She began to shake her head.

"How?" It was all she could manage to say.

"I don't know. They told me what to do and I did it. I did what you told me to do. I got better. They said I worked harder than any other patient ever. And, here I am."

"I don't believe it." Mikey was still trying to take in the image of this person in front of her. It was almost impossible to make the connection with him to John Doe. No, it was more like totally impossible to make the connection.

"Well, believe it or not, it's me. I thought you would be a little more happy to see me. It seemed that when I left you didn't want me to go. I thought… Maybe I was wrong. The man turned away and walked over to the sofa and sat down there not looking at her.

Mikey was still frozen with her eyes on him. He seemed bigger and much heavier. His dark hair had been cut short and his face had filled in. He was still pale. But, he showed no signs of the frail man that she had adopted as her friend. She stopped and focused on his face. He was *beautiful.* Mikey realized that she was really behaving badly. This *was* John Doe. Her friend. And, probably she was the only friend he had or at least could remember.

"I'm sorry." Mikey quickly walked over to the sofa and sat next to him.

"Wow. I am happy to see you. You have to forgive me. I almost didn't recognize you. You look great. And, I can't believe how well you are talking. You are walking! It is really amazing. How do you feel?"

"Good. No, really good now. Yea. It was really hard in the beginning, but it seemed to get much easier as it went on. First the talking and then the walking. Then the fitness and nutrition stuff. I feel like a whole new person now."

"And your memory?" Mikey was anxious to know if he had remember anything.

"No, that is the same. I've tried almost every day to remember anything. I just keep finding the same blank. It's frustrating. But, I have been learning how to do things and what things are and how they work. That stuff too."

"Like what?" Mikey was puzzled.

"Like the lights, the telephone, the television, hairdryers. Ha ha ha. Everything really." He laughed.

"You don't even remember those things?" Mikey was more puzzled.

"No. I only remember words. I didn't forget those. That was why it was so easy to start talking. But everything else is new."

"Wow. That has to be tough. I don't know how you are doing it. I really don't." Mikey was searching his person again for signs of familiarity.

"Oh, there is still a lot left. I know that. They told me that they were going to move me to a place where I could learn all this everyday stuff. It will be like my own place where I can practice all the things I need to know. They said there would be staff there in case I needed help. I only have to find a mentor first."

"What is a mentor?"

"Someone I can call if I just need some guidance or information. So, I gave them the name of the person I wanted to be my mentor." He looked directly at her and waited.

"Yea, well. Who is it?"

"You."

Mikey was stunned again. She sat there blinking.

"Me?"

"Well, yes. This is a person I have to trust to tell me the truth. I only know and trust one person out there. That's you. I trust you, Mikey." He sat there looking at her. His eyes were so deep and clear that they seemed to never end.

"I…don't…know. I mean, I don't know if that's okay. I mean, wouldn't they want a *man* to do that for you. I mean it seems a little inappropriate that a girl… I…" She stopped short trying to sort the whole thing out in her head before going on.

"Yea, that is what they said too. But, since my "case" is so unique, they decided that they may make an exception. They said that you were a police officer and would be able to get me onto the right path. So, they said it would be up to you." He sat there waiting for her answer.

"Okay. I think I have had it with all the surprises today. I am so confused right now. Would it be okay if I think about it? I mean, can I just have a little time to absorb all this? You know I want to help you in any way I can. I always have. I just feel a little overwhelmed. Please don't be upset. I am not saying no or anything yet. I just have to think it over." Mikey sat there trying to get a grasp on the whole morning.

"Okay. I understand. I remember what you said about possibly getting into trouble because of me. I don't want that. So, if you say no, I understand. They will find somebody to help me." He looked down and frowned.

"Yes, that is a problem for me. But, again. Please, just let me think about it. Okay?" Mikey was torn between running out the door this minute to get away or to reach out and take the hand of someone she felt so connected to. She resisted the urge to do either one. She was still in some control despite the chaos. She prided herself on that ability.

Suddenly the room was full of staff bringing lunch for the patient and scheduling the final round of testing that would approve John Doe's release to the assisted living facility. She greeted the staff as they came in but quickly noticed that their attention was solely on John Doe. Addie had been right about that part. Mikey chuckled to herself. Yep, she had definitely noticed too. He really was very *attractive*. It was such a transformation. However, at least she had the common sense to *control* herself. These nurses were comical approaching ridiculous. Well, he was in good hands now. She could excuse herself and crawl back to her house to figure this whole thing out.

Mikey stood up and no one even noticed. She cleared her throat and the crowd of nurses turned to look at her.

"Okay. Well, I really need to go now. I am glad to see how well the patient is doing. It is… something. I will check back in to see how things are going with you." Mikey smiled at them and John Doe and was turning to leave.

"When?" He quickly asked.

"Uh, I'll call you this evening. I noticed there's a phone on the night stand." Mikey nodded then continued turning and left the frenzied room to return to her quiet house to think. She laughed. It was funny that just 24 hours ago, she was finding ways to escape the confines of her house and now she was racing back to its safety. Life was always so strange. Stranger than fiction.

Mikey quickly entered the house. She felt exhausted. It was just after two p.m. and she really could use a nap. She felt a little too anxious to sleep. She went to the cabinet and poured herself a glass of her favorite nighttime beverage. Yes, she thought, it was much earlier than normal to start this. But, this had not been a normal day. So, all rules were off the table. She sipped the liquid and laid back onto the soft familiar comfort of her bed. She let her mind wander. Wow. This was just too much. She laughed out loud. Yes, she was totally sure that John Doe was an alien. She laughed even louder. Boy all those nurses would get a surprise when his antennae popped out now wouldn't they? Ha ha ha. She shook her head and pulled her hair from its updo. He was really something. She saw his face in her head. Although she mocked them, she understood what all the fuss was about. She had noticed it herself. Mikey closed her eyes tightly to push out any images.

"Don't even go there, Mikey." She chastised herself out loud. There were lines she did not want to cross. That was one of them. She built a very solid wall between herself and that image so that it did not enter her mind again. Mikey decided to take a quick nap and she would call Dorthea when she got up. She would think about all of the rest of the mess later when she had had a chance to unravel the mess her mind was in already.

"Hello, Dot?"

"Yes?"

"Hey, it's Mikey. How is everything? You getting ready for Christmas?" Mikey was anxious for the distraction of her endless chatter when questioned about anything.

"Uh, yea. Well, there are so many parties. I have work parties, house parties, and even several family parties. It is insane. My schedule is so crazy. But, I did call you back when I got your messages. Sorry. What's up?"

"Nothing. I just have a few weeks off. Forced vacation. I was hoping to get a chance to see you before the holiday and I *know* how quickly your calendar fills up! Ha ha ha." Mikey seemed to feel relaxed and comfortable despite the drama of the day. It made it easy to just chat with Dot. It felt good.

"Well, sure. I'd like that. You know what? There is this party and you could go with me. Plenty of people to meet Mikey. What a great idea... We could go shopping and find you something really cute to wear and..."

"Dot! Ok. I was thinking just getting together. Us. Me and you. That's it. You know I am not really good with people. I just wanted to find a night to hang out. That's all. No parties." Mikey was already slightly annoyed, but it seemed less than usual when she started this myriad of ulterior motives.

"Ok, ok. I was just thinking out loud. Ok, sure. But I have something going on until the 23rd. It that okay? Or, you could just come to the party!" Dorthea was proud of giving her the ultimatum.

"That will be fine. No parties." Mikey made a horrible face at the thought of shopping with Dorthea. She would have her parading around in things that looked like body socks all day. She winced at the mental picture.

"Alright. The 23rd it is. Really Mikey. You should think about what I am telling you, Miss Hermit Crab. It has been what? Maybe six years since you have been on a date. You sit there rotting. You are not getting younger. How old are you now? Let's see, if I am 28, that would make you… Three and four is…

"Thirty-seven. Yes, Dot, I am thirty-seven. Stop counting and put your shoe back on."

"You are mean Mikey. Really. I am just saying you are pushing the big FOUR ZERO here! Come on. When are you going to snap out of it? You are like a zombie. You never go anywhere and you dress like… well an old lady. No, you ARE a zombie. Geez. Would you have some fun already?"

"Dot. I am marking the 23rd on the calendar and hanging up now. BYE!"

There was so much more to think about that Mikey quickly discarded the memory of the phone call and the annoyance that came with it.

What to do about John Doe. That was the focal point now. Mikey sat quietly for several hours contemplating the risk involved. He was so amazing but was he worth risking everything she had worked for all these years? The case was closed and she could always deny "working" it like it was open. But, there would be questions about propriety. Misfeasance, malfeasance and nonfeasance were the words that came to her mind. There were the three terms that labeled "bad" cop behavior and lead to severe consequences. Singularly she had no idea what each one meant, but one thing was for sure. This could lead to one of these infractions, hell, maybe even two that would result in some kind of discipline. This was a serious decision. It was time to eat, but she really didn't feel like it. She would have to call him in a few hours. And, she knew he would be asking for her answer. She had to decide.

11

"orto San Francesco Hospital. How may I direct your call?"

"Yes, could I have room 1402 please?"

"Yes, please hold while I connect."

The phone rang three times.

"Hello?"

"Hello. It's Mikey. How are you holding up?"

"Mikey. I am doing good. Guess what?"

"What?" She feared some additional surprise that was going to kill her. She was at the limit.

"They said I can leave for the new place tomorrow. Isn't that great?" His voice was almost childlike in its transparent happiness.

"That is fantastic." Mikey wondered if he was really ready or the charitableness of the hospital was wearing thin.

"So, I guess I am getting my freedom starting tomorrow. Well some of it. I want to know everything Mikey. It feels like I just started living a few months ago. I feel like I missed the first part somehow. But I want to make up for it. I want… to get started already."

"Ha ha ha. Wow. That's great. I am so excited for you. I know you are going to do just fine. You have such a positive outlook that I am sure with a little time you will be *running* the hospital instead of being a patient there." Mike laughed and heard him laugh in return. It felt good.

"Did you think about it? I mean, what I asked you?"

Mikey knew the question was coming. She was prepared for it. She felt the plastic start to form around her mouth that slowly crept over her face and throat that signaled the calm even voice that would come out.

"Yes, I did. I thought a lot about it. I really did. I just think it is best that the hospital assign you a mentor for now. I will still be your friend and a part of your transition. I just think with work and everything, I may not be there if you need me. I don't want to let you down and leave you hanging when I can't just drop everything and help. So, I am kind of considering myself as your "unofficial mentor." Is that okay?"

There was a long pause on the line. She wondered if the plastic mask had smoothed the message sufficiently.

"Yes. That is okay. I met the man they assigned, Steve Reich. He seems nice and I think it will be great. I'll be lucky enough to have *two* mentors. Well, tomorrow is a big day. I am going to go to sleep now. I have a lot to remember so that I can do this. I am going to need to be ready for tomorrow. Good night, Mikey."

"Good night. Hey, I'll stop in tomorrow evening and check out the new place. Is that okay?"

"Yea, that would be nice. Goodbye." Click.

Mikey heard the disappointment in the voice that left her feeling a little queasy. This was the best path. It was best for him, best for her and the safest direction overall. It would be fine. None of that "feasance" stuff and she could still play a role in John Doe's life. A preferred role. His friend as opposed to some assignment. She would be there for him as long as he *wanted* her. Mikey was satisfied with her decision but still feeling the sting of the sadness in the voice of her new friend. She would definitely go tomorrow and see the new place. She would bring him a house-warming gift that was small until she saw what he really needed and surprise him with that later. It would be okay. She filled the empty glass and tried to find some comfort in it so she could sleep and get ready for tomorrow. She looked at the pile of unread books and laughed that she had wasted her money on them.

Mikey could tell that she slept late. It was so bright. The previous day had taken its toll on her in addition to the doubled amount of anesthetic from the night before. It was fuzzy and her head hurt. Great. She wobbled to the coffee pot. The empty pot felt heavy. It was going to be a long day. She filled the glass container and heaped the coffee into the basket. Thank God for caffeine. She went to the shower to pass the time until the pot was full of the black liquid that would help her regain some of her senses that the nightly amber one took away.

She came out of the shower and caught herself in the mirror. She stopped and looked for a moment and then shuddered at the image. She was okay for her age. But, there was always a hard edge that she hated when she saw herself. It definitely wasn't "girlish" at all. She started to laugh at herself. Well, it was bound to happen. You took a man's job and now you kind of resemble one. Just a little too tough to be clearly feminine. She recalled the image of John Doe and how amazing he looked now. She raised her eyebrows and wondered where the hell that thought came from. Who cared anyway? She pulled on the robe and went to find the coffee pot and a couple of aspirin.

Mikey did some house chores to pass the time and then went to the shopping center. She would have to put something together for John Doe's house-warming. God, where was Dorthea? What was she thinking? Dorthea would have turned this into some kind of menagerie of *themes* and *color schemes*. She was glad she resisted the urge to call her. Ouch. The thought hurt. Her mind turned to practicality. She would focus on that for now and once she saw what was there, she could do better at a later date. She decided to buy a laundry basket and fill it with items he may like or even experience for the first time. She smiled and went about filling the basket with unrelated items that she pictured him using but the facility not buying. Cologne, hair gel, body wash, gourmet coffee and cookies. Yes, this assortment was coming along. Dorthea would have died! Ha ha ha.

Great. Mikey was home and fumbling with the packaging. How long had it been since she had wrapped a package? Her mind went back and searched the past. Wow. It had been what? Eight or nine years already. It was so hard having lost them so soon. She had a little trouble picturing her parents at first. She was twenty-eight when a car accident had taken her family from her. Mother, father and brother in one instant – gone. She tried to remember what it was like before. She smiled It was so different from now. She belonged to something other than the department. She mumbled an obscenity and kept trying to mold the paper around the uneven object. Why didn't she just buy a toaster? A nice, easy box. She cursed at it again.

She followed the directions that Addison had given her. There was the parking lot. She pulled in and found a spot. She rolled her eyes at the rumpled package in the passenger seat. Whatever. She grabbed it and walked toward the building. The building seemed alright. Not new, but not run down. Hopefully the inside was as good. She got to the door. Locked. There was a buzzer system. Another obscenity. She scanned the mailboxes to find which apartment may be his. She scanned the list. Perfect. One was unlisted. None of the others were marked "Doe." She pushed the button.

"Yes?" The familiar voice was a relief.

She struggled with the package.

"Hi, it's Mikey."

"Hi. How are you?" The voice seemed cheerful. There was a slight pause.

"Great. Are you going to let me in?" She shifted the package again.

"Oh. yea. Right. Wait."

"There should be a button next to the inter...com"

The door buzzed before she could finish. Ha. She scanned the hall signs for number 17. Okay. Up one floor and to the... left. She followed the numbers and found the door. 17. She knocked with her foot balancing the heavy basket.

Click. The door opened. There he was. He was wearing a t-shirt and blue jeans. A definite improvement to the

hospital garb. Again, it was hard to digest. He looked…
She abandoned the thought and went in.

"Hi Mikey. I am so glad you came." He stood smiling

"Me too. I was so anxious to see your new place. Where can I put this?" It was getting heavy.

"What is it?" He seemed puzzed.

Okay, so it looked a little crazy and Mikey felt a little exasperated but determined.

"A present. Where can I put it?" God, how could just a few regular things be so heavy? Mikey thought.

"Oh, well anywhere is okay. A present? For what?" He was following behind her and she placed it on a small table just past the kitchen area.

"For you. For your new place. Nothing big. Just a little gift to well… to welcome you home." Mikey looked around. There was a small kitchen, dining nook, large livingroom and from what could be discerned a bathroom and bedroom. It was older but clean and adequate for now. The furniture was sparse and nothing on the walls. Her notes of the surroundings were complete.

Mikey turned to look at him. He stood staring at the rumpled object on the table. She was a little unnerved, but found her footing.

"So? Do you *like* it?" She was hoping to start some conversation.

"I don't know what it is." He looked puzzled.

"The apartment. Do you like it?"

"Yes! Yes I do. It is really nice. I keep walking around and looking at it. It's big."

Mikey laughed. Then she realized that comparatively speaking it was big to the one room area at the hospital. She nodded.

"Where is your mentor? What is his name?"

"Steve. He was here all day with me teaching me about all the things in here. We started at the door and went clockwise. I think I get it all. They are going to deliver some food tomorrow and I am going to learn how to *cook*. I am a little afraid of that. But, I have to do it. So, I am ready."

"That's great. Don't worry too much. Cooking is overrated. There is always frozen or take out." Mikey laughed at her own ineptness in that area. Maybe Steve could teach her a thing or two. She laughed.

"Well, I don't know how I'll do, but I guess it is sure important to be able to eat. It's first on the list. I have a television. Do you want to watch it with me?" He pointed to the living room area.

"Sure. That would be nice." She walked into the large living room. It was nice. Couch, chair, coffee table, lamps and TV. Basic, but good.

Mikey sat on the sofa and he went to turn on the TV. He seemed to be following steps in his head. It was cute. She laughed to herself.

He sat next to Mikey and picked up the remote control and began inspecting it.

"What do you want to see Mikey?"

"Whatever you want. I am going to let you pick. I don't normally watch TV. So, you find something for us to watch together." Mikey hated television. But, she would be sure to be entertained for his benefit.

He picked a cartoon. Mikey almost roared. It was so… perfect. So John Doe. They watched the characters perform their antics and laughed together. It was very easy to be there, Mikey thought. It was getting late and the radar in Mikey's head went off. Propriety.

"I should be going. It is getting late. Are you going to open my present?" She looked at the miserable lump still sitting on the table.

"What is it?" He was still a little hesitant about it.

"It is a present. You have to *open* it." She perceived that he wasn't getting the present concept. She grabbed his hand and took him to the table.

"It is just something I bought for you to celebrate your first day of freedom. It really isn't anything big. Just a gift for the occasion. Like birthdays, Christmas, weddings, and graduations. You buy the person something to make them happy. So, pull the paper off." Mikey pushed him toward the big colorful blob on the table. She laughed. It would scare her too.

"Open it how?" He was again puzzled.

She grabbed a piece and ripped it.

He looked shocked.

"The present is inside the paper. You can throw the paper part away." She realized that he had never experienced a present before. She felt a pang. That was sad.

He carefully pulled the paper apart to reveal the contents and seemed to come alive.

"Mikey! It is great. That is for me?"

"Yep. Like I said. Nothing spectacular or anything. I just wanted to get you something to celebrate your first day here. I didn't know what you needed." Mikey felt awkward. Maybe she really should have consulted Dorthea.

"That is so great. I love it all. Thank you." He carefully went through the items and was slowly identifying the packages. He stopped and spun around and looked at her. He lunged forward and grabbed her so tightly that she couldn't breathe. He was so much stronger than she had anticipated and was fighting back the urge push away. Finally he eased on the grip. Mikey was fairly sure that this was going to leave a mark. She felt the heat in her upper rib cage that signaled the beginnings of a bruise. She quickly pulled the plastic smile together.

"Mikey, this is my first present. Thank you." He looked so happy. So warm. So vulnerable. She didn't know whether to kiss him or pray for him.

"I am so honored to have given it you." She reached up and touched his cheek and smiled. It was fun. Thank you for sharing your first night with me. She smiled and walked to the door.

"Okay. I'll call to check in on you tomorrow. Do you still have my card with my cell on it?"

He gestured to the table.

"Ok, well call me if you need anything. Have a good night." She waved and left.

Walking to her car, she mused at how contagious John Doe was. He had almost broken through her walls. *Almost* was the key word. She was darting down the familiar streets to get home and digest her visit with John Doe. She pulled into the drive and went inside.

Mikey was still amazed that he didn't know about presents. She decided that his mentor, Steve, could take care of teaching him his daily routine. She wanted to get him outside to see everything. She still had ten vacation days left. She would make the most of the time off while she had it. Mikey decided to make a list of all the things in the city she wanted to show him. It would begin tomorrow. Maybe just a tour of the city. It was almost Christmas and the lights in some areas were really great. Mikey was proud of her plan and went to bed.

Mikey slept late. She followed the usual routine by heading straight for the coffee pot. After several cups, she decided to print out a map of the city and note several places to drive to this evening. She was really looking forward to it. She felt anxious. She decided to call Dorthea. She needed to solidify their plans for the end of this week. Mikey grabbed her phone and dialed the number. The phone rang only once.

"Hello?" there was a lot of noise in the background.

"Hello. Dot. Can you hear me?"

"Hello?"

"DOT! CAN YOU HEAR ME?" Mikey yelled into the phone.

"Oh yea. Hey Mikey. I really can't talk. We are at the stadium up north. We went to the hockey exhibition. Me and some girls from work. You should be here. Some of these guys are so hot!"

"Okay. I just wanted to know where we were going to dinner Friday. Any suggestions?"

"Oh yea. That's right. I almost forgot. How about Filomenas?"

"Okay, sounds good. I'll make the reservations tomorrow. Have fun!

"Bye."

Dot was always doing *something*. Did she ever stay home? Mikey went to the closet and picked out some warmer clothes to wear today. It was definitely getting colder. And, if she was going to be outside on a tour of the city, she would need something warmer. Wait? Did John Doe have something warm enough? She pulled out her cell and dialed his apartment.

"Hello?"

Not a voice that Mikey recognized. It must be the mentor.

"Hello. May I speak to… John?" Mikey hated saying that name out loud. It really wasn't his name. She avoided it very chance she could.

"Yes, who is calling?"

"This is Mikey." Wow, this guy was nosey, Mikey thought. Maybe just protocol.

"Hello, Mikey."

Now that was the voice she was looking for.

"Hi. I just wanted to ask you a question. Do you have any warm winter clothes and a coat? Maybe even a hat? I was thinking of taking you out this evening for a city tour. If that is okay with you?"

"I have to ask Steve. Hold on."

Heard a loud clunk as he laid the phone on the table. Mikey was pulling things out of her closet while she waited for him to return.

"Hello?"

"Yea, I'm still here." Mikey was searching for shoes at the bottom of the closet while awkwardly keeping the phone to her ear.

"He said yes on the clothes, but I guess there is something about rules. He asked me if you could stop by here today before he left. He leaves at four."

Mikey looked at her watch. There was plenty of time to do her house chores and get there by three.

"Sure. I'll be there at three. Okay?"

"That is great. I'll see you in a while, Mikey."

Mikey rushed through her chores and it was soon time to make her way to the Central District. She pulled into the lot and rang the buzzer. The door clicked and she went inside. She knocked on the door and he opened it.

"Hi Mikey!" He was smiling so hard it looked like his face would break.

"Hi. May I come in?"

"Oh, yea. Ha. I forgot that part again. Sorry."

"No problem." Mikey walked into the apartment and smiled at the man sitting at the dinette. She walked over to him.

"Hi. I am Mikey. Well, Michela Solitro. I take it that you are Steve?" Mikey extended her hand to the man seated at the table.

The man got up and took her hand while eyeing her suspiciously.

"Yes, Steve Reich. I am the mentor assigned to John. He mentioned that his girlfriend was coming to pick him up today and take him somewhere. Well, Miss, there are some rules in this living facility."

Mikey opened her mouth to speak but Steve quickly held up one finger in front of her at face level and continued.

"Now, John is here to learn about daily life, but we do not advocate outsiders interfering with out patients' recovery. We also do not allow outsiders to remain on the premises after eleven p.m. In addition, we also must clear our residents to be removed from the facility. Even with permission, they must be returned to the facility before eleven p.m. I am still not sure how he has met a girlfriend given his history, so I will be watching this situation very closely." He stood close and was glaring at her.

Mikey was completely astonished and stood there with her mouth open for another second. She regained her composure and looked directly at the man with a steel gaze.

"Ok, now that your speech is over, I will respond. You must not have checked your patient's file very carefully if you don't know who I am as it is clearly detailed in it. For the record, I am not Mr. Doe's *girlfriend*. I am his *friend*. Surely you can understand his referencing me as a girl AND a friend given his diagnosis. I was the detective assigned to his case after his accident and was therefore the only person outside the hospital that he knew. Maybe he used the term, but we both understand that a lot of things are new to him and maybe you should have ascertained the details *before* you began jumping to conclusions. And, I was actually the first person asked to be his mentor but declined due to the gender issues you seem to be eluding to. I thought it best for a male to be assisting him in his daily routine. But, I do plan on being involved in his recovery. I can make a phone call to Addison O'Neill right now if you need any clarification on that." Mikey's voice was quite forceful. She wanted to make herself clear. She looked at John Doe whom she forgot was standing there. The look on his face could only be described as totally lost.

"I'm sorry. I didn't mean to upset you." Mikey took the several steps that separated them. She reached out and patted his shoulder.

He stared at her for a minute and the look seemed to lessen. Mikey felt a little better.

She turned to the man she had been speaking to. He seemed to soften his position as well.

Miracle

"I'm sorry. I didn't know that you were the detective from the hospital. John just said his girlfriend was taking him out. I was only looking out for him. I thought maybe someone had come here trying to take advantage of him or something. Yes, I do know who you are now. Can we start over?" He looked sincerely at her.

"Sure. I am hoping that we can actually work together. I just wanted to take him out for a tour of the city. I thought he might enjoy getting familiar with his surroundings as well as see some Christmas lights. Maybe the pier? That is it. But, if we were to do any walking, he would need a jacket. That was why I called today."

"Oh yes, he has everything he needs for something like that. No problem. I know he is in good hands. Well, John. You have a nice evening planned. I hope you enjoy it. I can leave early since your friend is here and I'll see how it went when I get here in the morning. Is that okay?"

"Okay Steve. See you tomorrow." John Doe still had not moved and was still looking at Mikey.

Mikey looked up at him and noticed the still strange look on his face.

"What's wrong?"

"I have never seen you act like that before. You are always nice. I was surprised. It didn't sound like you."

Mikey felt sorry she let her temper get away from her.

"I am always nice to *you*. Yes, but I am not always nice. That is the truth. You have to remember that I am a detective. I can be quite a jerk when I want to be. That had nothing to do with you. I just didn't like the accusations that they guy was making. Like I would come here to *do something* to you. How ridiculous. I am not trying to hurt

167

you." Mikey was mumbling obscenities softly under her breath.

"I know that, Mikey." He walked over to the table and sat in the chair that Steve had just vacated.

"Okay. Well, what do you want to do? We can get an early start if you like or we could stay here for a while and go later. It is up to you." Mikey went to the table and sat next to him trying to change the tone hanging in the air.

"Let's go. I am ready to get out of here." He smiled at her and the moment relaxed and returned to normal.

Mikey pulled out of the apartment lot and had her map on the console between them.

"I figured that I would show you around and mark places you would need to know on it. We can also mark places that you want to go on it. Maybe even keep track of places we have been. So, let's start with the hospital."

Mikey took her time and drove much more slowly than usual. She wanted him to see his surroundings and get his bearings in the city. She stopped in front of the hospital, police station, post office, a grocery store, department store and pharmacy near the apartment. They found the locations on the map together and marked each one with a number and wrote the corresponding name on a list beneath the map. Although the activity was functional, it was filled with light-hearted conversation. It was refreshing for Mikey. She hadn't felt herself laugh so easily for a very long time. She enjoyed seeing the city through his fresh outlook. She never realized how cynical she had become until now. It was getting late and the Christmas lights would have to wait for another day. But, there was still enough to enjoy a little time on the pier. The crisp night air and sound of the waves were always nice at night.

Mikey and her tourist walked along the pier and stopped to lean upon one of the large posts.

"It is so dark out there. It reminds me of the beginning. The part I can remember. It was just like that. Dark. But there wasn't a breeze or the sound of the waves. Just the dark." He seemed lost in thought for a long while after he spoke.

Mikey wondered what that all had been like. Now she could understand it a little bit. She reached out and clasped his hand. He must have really felt so alone then. It really was dark out there. It was scary when she looked at it that way. They just stood together quietly in the crisp night air. His hand was so warm.

"Well, I hate to spoil the evening, but it is ten thirty. I guess we should be getting back before we break Steve's rules." Mikey squeezed his hand to break his trance.

"Why don't you ever say my name?" he said it without moving and still staring into the darkness.

Mikey was a little shocked by the question and briefly thought about denying it until she realized that he was right.

"Well, because I still don't *know* what your name is. John Doe is so generic. It doesn't really define who you are. I guess that's why." Mikey had trouble saying the words. She wasn't used to having to be so completely honest. It made her feel vulnerable. That was something she tried to avoid.

"I understand that. But, it bothers me a little that you never seem to talk directly to me -when you avoid my name. At least the only name I know right now." He finally turned to look at her.

She could understand that. She just wished she had been able to figure out who he was so that she could have given him the information that he needed. But, she figured he was right. She did have to call him something. *He* and *You* wouldn't last forever.

"Okay. Okay, John. You're right. I will change that. I didn't mean to hurt your feelings. Okay?" She squeezed his hand again to reassure him that she meant it.

John smiled at her.

"Thank you. Can I ask you something else?"

"Sure, why not?" She couldn't believe there was more. She braced herself.

"Do you mind if I start calling you Michela?" He looked at her again.

"No, I don't mind. It is my name. Mikey is just something that started at the department a long time ago and it stuck. I really hated it at first, but I just got used to it over the years. I even use it myself all the time now. But, no. I actually like being called Michela." She thought back for a minute to the years she had spent with Kyle. He never called her Mikey. He hated the name as well. He said he always worried that if someone didn't know her, they would think he was with another man. Ha ha ha. But, she did remember that she liked the sound of it when Kyle would say it. Gosh, that was so long ago. Okay, time was wasting and it was almost eleven.

"Are you ready? We are going to miss your curfew… John." She smiled at him mocking the emphasis she placed on the word John. He released her hand and they walked back to the car. They spent the ride back to the apartment talking about where they could go the following day. Maybe the shopping center. It was big and would take up several hours. They agreed. She dropped him off at the building and waved as he went inside. The ride home seemed so quiet. She felt a little pang of sadness. She missed him already. It was going to be a long night.

12

Mikey slowly got out of bed. She yawned and her feet began the walk to the coffee maker before her mind could catch up. She found herself at the kitchen counter. This vacation thing was growing on her. Water in the pot-coffee in the basket. She perched herself on the stool at the counter and waited. What day was it? Friday. Where had the week gone? She smiled. She had been to the shopping center one day and the video arcade the next. Each night she would take John to the pier. He seemed to really like the nights there. What would they do today? Wait? What day was it? Friday the 23rd. Shit. Dinner with Dot. She had forgotten all about it. And, to make the reservations. She muttered a few words to herself. What time was it? What time did Filomena's open? She started fumbling for the phone book in the drawer. There it was. She sat still for a moment. What about John? She had not mentioned that she had plans tonight. Would she hurt his feelings if she didn't go with him today? She would surely piss off Dorthea if she canceled. That was for sure. Which was worse? She pondered for a moment. Equal. She dialed the phone.

"Filomena's Ristorante. May I help you?"

"Yes, I needed to make a reservation for tonite. Is there anything open?" Mikey winced waiting for the answer.

"Yes, I have one table left. Your name please."

"Michela Solitro."

"How many?"

Mikey hesitated.

"Three." She said in more of a question than a statement.

"Okay, Ms. Solitro. I have a table for three for seven p.m. Is that okay?"

"I guess so. Last one. Thank you so much." Mikey hung the phone up. She figured if she chickened out in taking John Doe to meet Dorthea, they wouldn't care if two showed up instead of three. It kept the bases covered for now until she could think. The coffee was almost ready. She groaned imagining Dorthea's reaction. She also didn't like the thought of having to share John's attention. Surely Dorthea would monopolize the entire evening. She could suffer through one night. She didn't feel like getting the barrage of questions so she decided to keep John a surprise. She would call Dot and have her meet them at the restaurant at seven. She sipped the fresh, hot coffee. She groaned again. What the hell was she going to wear? Filomena's was a little upscale. Did John have anything to wear? Dorthea was such a critic. She was going to have to call Steve again. She grabbed her cell phone and began dialing. Mikey was sure this evening was going to necessitate a trip to the shopping mall. Just great. Two days before Christmas. The image of a thousand people and buggies made her eyes want to bleed. Ugh. Mikey flinched.

❖

Mikey arrived at John's apartment promptly at six o'clock. She carried the jacket, shirt and tie she bought along with the black dress she was wearing. She hoped Steve was right in guessing John's size. There was no margin for error. They should go okay with the tan khakis that Steve described in John's closet. Steve seemed more excited about the night than John. She walked toward the door to press the buzzer. He was usually so eager to go out. It seemed odd that he told her he thought they could just stay in tonight. Maybe he wasn't feeling well. All of this was so new. She kept forgetting that. Maybe all of it was overwhelming. She would double check that he felt up to going once she got inside. The door clicked and she pulled it open with one finger while clutching the remaining items in her hands. She walked to the door and softly gave it a quick knock.

The door opened and Mikey was smiling, anxious to see him. He half smiled and opened the door.

"Hi John." She watched him intently for his reaction.

"Hi Michela. What all do you have there?" He seemed curious to look.

"Well… I told you I was going to get you the rest of your clothes for tonight. So, here they are. I hope you like them and I really hope they fit. I am so sorry for forgetting about my plans for tonight. I told you that Dorthea is my friend. I don't want to disappoint her. And, I don't want to miss an evening with you. So, this was my best solution. Hey look. If you don't want to go, I'll understand. Are you feeling alright? Is this all getting to be too much all at once?"

"No. I mean yes. Well, Yes I feel fine. And, no this isn't too much. I had just planned a night for us to relax here. That's all. I forget too. You know, that you have a life outside of this apartment. I am sorry too. I should have asked you before I planned my evening. I'm still getting used to the rules of friendship and stuff. It will be great. Maybe I will enjoy tonight anyway. I am going to try to do that." He smiled at her.

"Good. Thank you for understanding. Now, let's get you into all of this and see how it goes." Mikey started to remove the items from the garment bags. T-shirt, shirt, jacket, tie and clasp. Yes, she had it all. Before she could hand them to him, he immediately jerked off the t-shirt he was wearing and stood there waiting. Mikey stood frozen for a moment looking at him just standing there. He was still pale and lean, but surprisingly muscular. As he reached for the shirts, his muscles moved under his skin. She quickly looked away and turned her back while he proceeded to put the first item on. She walked over and turned on the television set and removed her long coat and sat down. She quickly needed a distraction to keep her mind from dwelling on the image. The weather channel. Perfect. They were talking about frontal systems. She changed the channel.

"How does it look?" John stood there in the new shirt.

"Not too bad. You have to tuck it in though. Into your pants." She quickly looked back at the TV in case he decided to unassembled himself in front of her again. No way was she going to look until it was safe. She took a deep breath.

"Okay. Now, how does it look?" He stood there again waiting for her approval.

"Great. Now you need the tie." She was relieved. The worst was over.

"Here it is. Now what do I do with it?" He stood there holding the tie.

"Shit." Panic had returned. Mikey had no idea how to tie a tie. She was now panic-stricken. She hadn't thought of this.

Thankfully, John produced a piece of paper with Steve's cell phone number on it. They called him praying that he would answer.

"Hello?"

Steve began laughing as Mikey started to babble about the tie issue. It wasn't funny to her. At all. He then started laughing so hard that she gave the phone to John and marched into the livingroom. This was going to be a long night. What had she been thinking? She could hear John saying 'Okay, then what?' about a hundred times in the kitchen. After what seemed to be an eternity he came into the livingroom.

"How does this look?" He stood there proudly with what appeared to be the perfectly tied tie. Mikey wanted to ask how he could have possibly done that from directions over the phone. She didn't have time. She would try to remember to ask him later. She yanked the jacket off of the chair and thrust it out to him. He quickly slid it on.

She stepped back and looked at him. He looked great. She smiled.

"Am I okay?" He was questioning himself looking at his sleeves and then back at her.

"You look very nice. We are going to be late if we don't hurry." She rolled her eyes and they laughed walking toward the door.

Mikey squeeled the tires turning into the lot of Filomena's. She hated being late. She parked in the first open spot. They jumped out and walked quickly to the front door.

"Yes?"

"Good evening. Table for Michela Solitro."

"Yes, party of three. Your other party arrived just about five minutes ago. I will seat you and then go and get her from the lounge."

"Thank you." Mikey and John followed the older man to a corner table with three chairs. They sat and waited for the remaining party. John seemed to fidget a little. Mikey wondered why he was nervous.

"There you are! Mikey you are never late. I thought something happened... to... you..." Her eyes settled upon John Doe. She was not doing a good job of hiding her surprise and her subsequent intense scan of him as he stood to greet her. Not subtle at all. Mikey felt a little irritated and smug at the same time.

"Dorthea, I would like you to meet my friend, John. John this is Dorthea." Mikey was smiling, but was a little nervous too.

"Well, isn't this a surprise? Nice to meet you. Is this *John Doe*?" Dorthea flashed the million dollar smile that came so naturally to her. She slid off her coat to reveal a very *small* black dress that revealed her youthful figure.

"Yes, it is." Mikey felt instantly uncomfortable and awkward standing there.

"It is so nice to meet you, Dorthea. I have heard so much about you. Mikey said you were pretty. I didn't give you enough credit." John Doe smiled at Dorthea and Mikey was in awe. He was actually *lying*. She hadn't said two words about Dorthea until today. What was this? She felt an uncomfortable knot begin to form in her stomach.

Dorthea quickly snatched the chair next to the focus of her attention and Mikey sat across the table from them. Aw, she expected this. She would be the perfect spectator for the next several hours. She *knew* Dorthea. Whatever. What did she care anyway? Maybe Dorthea and John Doe would hit it off and Dot could finally stop searching the planet for the perfect man. Yea, she thought while she played with the food that had just arrived with her fork. He was pretty perfect. That was clear during the shirt changing incident. What was she thinking anyway? How old was John Doe? She looked up at him engrossed in conversation with Dot. He looked more her age. She exhaled and continued to play with her food and nod when either of them acknowledged her. She began to think this was a mistake. But, probably not. It would have happened eventually when John got out into the world. Wasn't that what she wanted anyway? She was his *co-mentor*. She wasn't supposed to want him to stay shackled inside the assisted living cubicle. Although it was a nice thought. She stopped that train of thought squarely in its tracks. What to pretend to have for dessert? She decided to pick the first thing on the menu. It didn't matter. She looked out the window and tried to smile.

The waiter arrived with the check. Dorthea gestured at Mikey. Mikey dutifully accepted it and quickly calculated twenty percent and scribbled the numbers on the paper and handed the stoic man the slip and her debit card. He thanked her and was off. Thank God this was almost over. She was ready to go home. She would have ordered at least one drink after dinner but she was driving John Doe and it seemed irresponsible. She could wait to numb some of this until she got home. She looked up and the man had returned with the receipt. She thanked him and tried to tune into the current conversation.

"Well, I must say that Mikey has got to bring you around more often. I have so many people I would like you to meet. She has been selfish keeping you to herself." Dorthea reached her hand over to place it on John Doe's hand on the table. Mikey rolled her eyes before she could catch herself.

"Yes, well. I leave the social planning to Michela. But, it would be really nice to see you again Dorthea." He smiled so warmly at her.

Mikey could barely contain the word "yuck" from coming out of her mouth aloud.

"Please call me Dot, now that we are friends, John."

Mikey thought the syrup would flood the room. She clenched her teeth and smiled.

"Sure, Dot. I am sure we will see each other again. Thank you for a really nice evening." He stood up and helped Dorthea to her feet. Then he assisted her with her coat. Mikey was amazed. Hell, he couldn't even remember to let her in the door when she buzzed. She held her breath to keep from groaning out loud. She smiled dutifully as they hugged each other good night and made their parting greetings. She was wiggling into her coat and collecting her bag. She pretended not to notice that Dot still had a hold of his hand. She turned and raised an eyebrow.

Mikey and John walked into the brisk air to make it to the parked car. Mikey got into the driver's seat and waited until he had positioned himself and latched the seatbelt. She put the car in reverse and began driving back to the Central District. She didn't utter a sound for several miles.

"Your friend is very nice. Quite talkative." He quietly broke the silence that seemed to hang in the air.

"Yes, she is." Mikey didn't take her eyes off the road and didn't offer anything further.

The drive would take about thirty minutes and Mikey decided she could cut that to twenty if she broke the limit a little. She stepped on the gas.

"Michela. I am actually not ready to go home yet. I was going to ask you earlier, but with the tie and all, I was distracted. I want to go to one other place before we head back. Would that be okay?" He was looking at her. She could feel it. But, she did not look over. She glanced down at the clock on the dashboard. 9:05 p.m.

"Where is that?" She flatly responded.

"I want to see where you live."

Mikey felt her foot slip off the gas pedal with the jerk her body made.

"What?" She glanced over at him. He was looking at her but she couldn't look long enough to read his face.

"I want to see where you live. I have the map in my pocket. You said we could go to places I needed and wanted. Well, I would like to know where you live."

She scowled – frozen, looking forward. It seemed a ridiculous request at the moment.

"It is getting late, John. I am not sure we have enough time. Maybe we could plan it another day." She was making an excuse so she could just get him home.

"Michela. Please?"

His voice was so soft and seemed to plead his case. Maybe it would be good to know. If he got lost or something. He should know where to go if he found himself in the neighborhood. Fine she thought.

"Ok, sure. But just for a little while, an hour. I have to get you back before eleven." Mikey made a quick evasive lane change to exit the freeway since she was now going in the wrong direction. She exited and made several quick turns and pulled into her driveway. It seemed weird to have him there. She shrugged off the feeling and put the plastic face on, exited the car and walked quickly to her door. She thought she could take a minute to change before driving him home. She was cold.

They entered the small two-story house. Michela switched on the lights and walked to the livingroom and turned on the TV. She couldn't remember the last time it had been on.

"Hey, would you like something to drink?" She started searching for the remote control. Where the hell was it?

"Sure." He walked in behind her.

Ha. There it was. She handed him the remote.

"What would you like?" She started thinking about the contents of her refrigerator. Bottled water, maybe one can of ginger ale. Was there some kind of juice in there? She was unprepared for this. She felt a little self-conscious.

"I'll have what you are having." He shrugged.

"Oh, well, she started to laugh. I usually only have a cocktail at night so I don't keep much here." She started to go over the list of the refrigerator contents again.

"That would be fine."

"What?" She continued to look in the mostly empty appliance for the juice she *swore* was in there.

"A cocktail. I'd like that."

Mikey spun around from the lit compartment to look at him. He was now standing in the kitchen.

"You want what? No, I don't think so. I mean, I am supposed to be showing you the *good* stuff and I don't know about your medical condition. That is really not a good idea. No way." Mikey was now shaking her head in the negative.

"What? Michela. I am fine. I am not taking any pills or anything. I *told* you that I wanted to know everything. So, I want to try it. So what? Why are you looking at me like that? Do you think I am a *child*?" He started to seem insulted. Mikey felt sheepish about her motherly reaction.

"No. I know you are not a child. Like I said. I just..." Mikey shrugged for a lack of anything else to say.

He stood there waiting. She felt a little pressured and unsure of the whole thing. She looked at him. He seemed determined. She sighed out loud. Whatever. She would surely be fired from mentoring. She heaved another sigh and started for the upstairs. Mikey walked to her bedroom. It was actually the entire upstairs except for the bathroom. It contained a sitting area and TV along with her bedroom furniture. She went to the cabinet and pulled out a glass and poured a single shot into it. She turned to go back down and was startled that he had followed and was standing behind her. She jumped slightly.

"You scared me." Mikey blinked a few times and handed John the glass he had requested.

Mikey watched John Doe mull around the room looking at her wall hangings and then the stack of unread books she had on the night stand. He sat on the bed and began inspecting the titles. Mikey felt a little violated. No one had been in this room for so many years. It was weird. She tried to just ignore it.

"Okay. Well, make yourself at home. I am going to go change and then I can take you home."

"Why?" He jerked and looked up at her.

"Why what?" Mikey was getting a little tired from the whole evening. She felt a little foggy.

"Change? You look so nice. I have tried to imagine you in different places before. But, I never imagined you like this. You look really good." He had become even more serious and stood up.

"Thanks. Well, I don't usually dress…" She trailed off as he began walking toward her.

Mikey couldn't look at him now. He was too close and she feared he would see the stupid jealousy she had felt earlier. She was so dumb. She waited for him to ask her some stupid question that would redirect the thoughts she had all night. She decided to redirect it herself.

"So? You really liked Dorthea? Wow. I hadn't thought of that or I would have introduced you sooner. You both really seemed to hit it off." Mikey continued to stare off away from him. It was so immature, but she couldn't help it.

"Yes. She was very nice. Very *friendly*. I wouldn't have pictured her like that. I thought she would be more like you."

God, he was so close. She nervously started fixing her hair and shifting from one foot to the other.

"Oh no. Dot and I are total opposites. We always have been." It was good to talk about something else, even if it was Dorthea.

"Yes, I see that."

Mikey wondered if somehow he had gotten even closer without her knowing it. It was getting hard to breathe. Maybe she was John Doe's friend, but she wasn't feeling friend-like right now. This was too close. She decided that it was time to go.

"Okay. I'll make sure the two of you get to spend more time together. It is time I took you back. Mikey turned to walk away. She could have barely completed one step before feeling a tight grip upon her wrist and the propulsion of being spun and pulled backward. Mikey found herself face-to-face against John Doe. She held her breath.

His chest felt so hard against hers. Where were her bricks? She was trying to put the wall back up.

"Michela. I don't want to spend more time with Dorthea. Is that why you are acting so strange?" He wrapped his arms around her waist so that she couldn't escape. When the hell did he get so strong? She tried to move but it wasn't working.

"You seemed to get along with her just fine. She really seemed to like you too." The words were cold.

"Michela. Michela?"

Mikey still didn't look at him.

"The dinner was your idea. I told you I had something else planned. But, I didn't want to ruin your night. So, I did what you wanted. Now I want to do what I had planned. Ha. What I had been planning all week. I wanted a night alone with *you*."

Mikey was starting to be overcome with the voltage of electricity she felt in her body. It was fight or flight. She increased the pressure her hand was placing against his chest.

"Stop it." Mikey managed to blurt out while her mind was trying to calculate this situation.

"I am not here to *teach* you this." She plead with him as she clenched her eyes tightly shut.

"I don't want you to *teach me* anything. I want to know you. Let me show you me. Let me show you." He was almost whispering in her ear. God, she was almost feeling drunk without one single drop of the nightly serum.

"John, please. You don't want this. It will change things." She tried hard again to move without any success.

"I have wanted this since the first time I heard your voice calling me when I was in the dark. It was how I got through all those months at the rehab center. It was why I asked to come back here. It was why I had them call you. I have wanted this moment for as long as *I* can remember. Michela, please. I want this. I want to know what this feels like. I want that with you. Please let me touch you."

Mikey stopped pushing against his chest. And, in that exact moment her strength disappeared and she began trembling. She couldn't make it stop. A loud gasp came from her mouth that she felt start in her feet and run the length of her body. She had completely lost this battle. She was sure she would be sorry about it tomorrow.

Mikey pulled closer to the man in front of her. Her breath came in jagged spurts and she felt completely alive for the first time in so long. His hands were so warm on her skin. She couldn't tell whose breaths were louder now. It didn't really matter. Like him, she finally admitted that she wanted this. There was no turning back now or to undo what was already in motion.

13

The morning light was coming into the bedroom window. Mikey started to become conscious. Her body felt in an awkward position and Mikey tried to stretch until she bumped into the body lying next to hers. She froze and searched her foggy mind. The images were slow at first but then it all flooded back to her now fully awake mind. She was afraid to open her eyes. Was it were all real or only a dream? Each left positive and negative consequences. She decided to move when she was well aware of the stiffness in all of her joints. The little detective section of her brain shouted "REAL!" inside her head. She now heard the sound of soft breathing next to her. At least he was alive. From the compilation of images she had gathered up in her head, they should probably *both* be *dead*. Wow. He sure did show her something. Where *did* he learn that?

Mikey halted her wandering mind. She slowly opened her eyes and turned to the source of the soft sound next to her. He was sound asleep. She hadn't awoken him. She was still so amazed at how beautiful he was. She slipped off the side of the bed and tip-toed to the kitchen and the familiar plastic appliance that would soon provide her some needed energy. Maybe an aspirin too. She ached all over. Mikey went to the bathroom to get a shower. Coffee would be done when she was finished. The warm water felt great on her aching muscles.

Mikey finished quickly and was enroute to the kitchen. She stopped suddenly when she discovered he was sitting at the counter on the stool in her usual spot. He didn't say anything and just looked at her. She felt fairly self-conscious and began fumbling with the long mass of wet hair. She felt her cheeks getting hot and it only added to the miserable self-awareness she was feeling.

"Good morning." He stood up and went to the cabinets and began looking inside them. He found two cups and poured the black liquid in each one. He handed one to her.

"Thanks." Mikey nervously smiled and walked up to him to take the cup.

"Did I wake you? I tried to be quiet." Mikey wanted to break the silence that was making her uncomfortable.

"No. Not at all. I just woke up and you weren't there. I came looking for you." He began smiling at her and reached out to her free hand. He pulled her closer.

"Michela."

Mikey put her arms around his neck and her head on his shoulder. It felt nice.

"Last night was amazing. It was so much better than I had imagined. I am really glad you changed the plans. It was all so perfect here with you. Thank you." He was stroking her cheek and wet hair.

Mikey was so content just standing there. She never wanted to move. Wait… Something he said was bothering her. Here. Oh crap. He was still here!!! What about the curfew. Surely they had reported him as a missing person by now. Steve probably came and found him gone. Oh Great!

"John." Mikey jerked upright.

"I have to get you back. Oh, I am sure they have already realized you didn't come back last night. Oh God. How am I going to explain this? A flat tire? Oh no. Steve will surely rat me out on this one. Hurry up, get dressed." Mikey was already throwing items into her purse preparing to leave as quickly as possible.

"Hey, it's okay. He knows where I am. I was released from that restriction yesterday."

Mikey turned to look at him waiting for further explanation.

"When you called and changed the plans. Well, *my* plans, I talked to Steve about it. I showed him the map and all the places we have been. He understood and released me from the curfew." John smiled.

Mikey half frowned thinking about it.

"What exactly did you talk to Steve about?" Mikey was now a little uncomfortable.

"Everything. He had helped me plan for the night at the apartment then he was able to get my status changed. He said it was my Christmas gift. He is even trying to find me a job. Steve is great." John seemed happy about all of this as he sat there smiling.

Mikey raised one eyebrow and then both. Great. This was not a *secret*. Double Great. Nothing she could do about it now. She plopped onto the stool next to John and began sipping the coffee with her eyes closed.

She managed to get John to take his shower and she zipped through the house tidying up after last night. She laughed. There were clothes everywhere. How did two people make such a mess? She assembled some sense of order and grabbed something to wear.

Mikey went back to the kitchen. Not much in the fridge. She should get him something to eat since there was no urgency now that she had not committed some kind of violation. Sort of. He was soon ready and they were deciding on the day's activities. It was Christmas Eve. Surely the stores would be a mess. They agreed no gifts. John didn't want Mikey to buy anything since he wasn't able to get her anything in return.

They ate leisurely at a small local restaurant. The talk focused mostly on John's excitement for the future. He was so anxious for Steve to get him a job so he could feel productive. He felt very optimistic that he was going to make record progress just so he could be on his own and get to living his own life. Mikey had no doubts. He seemed to accomplish whatever he set his mind on. The shopping center was a mad house. They walked along the storefronts talking, enjoying the Christmas music and people watching. Mikey never failed to be amazed at his perceptions of people and things. He had a simplistic yet insightful view on so many things. It was sometimes hard to believe this was the man she met in the hospital that first day. It wasn't hard to understand why she liked him so much. His company was like fresh air compared to the thick smog she was used to inhaling. They found a photo booth and laughed while taking several photos of themselves.

They decided to head back to the apartment. There were so many Christmas specials on television and John was anxious to see them all. Mikey laughed. She never imagined spending Christmas Eve and probably Christmas day engrossed in holiday classics. But, she reasoned that it would be fun just to watch his delight at all the heart-warming stories. They began the walk back.

Although the streets were noisy, it would have been impossible to miss the sound of a woman screaming over the crowd.

"Freddie. Freddie!" It was so loud. They both turned to see where the source of the shrieking was coming from. Not far away there was some ragged looking woman running in their direction. She was getting closer.

Mikey made a quick assessment of this character. Dirty and disheveled. Mikey saw she was running straight in their direction and assumed a protective stance in front of John. Mikey waited for the woman to pass by, but instead she stopped dead in front of them. The smell of alcohol emanating from this wild-eyed woman was almost toxic.

"Freddie. Is that YOU? Freddie, I thought I'd never see ya again. I had no idea where they'd taken ya. I looked. I did. What? Don't ya know me?" The woman looked hard at John with her wild bloodshot eyes.

Mikey was careful to remain in front of John who seemed stunned by it.

"Freddie. It's *me*, Annie. I knew you were alive. I just KNEW it." She was trying to inch closer and Mikey stepped forward with her arm outstretched.

"Okay, lady. Calm down. What do you want?" Mikey had turned to hard plastic. One hand on John. One hand in defense of the nut in front of her.

The woman just stared at the man behind her with her half focused eyes.

"Lady. I am going to ask you one more time. Do you need help?" Mikey's position hadn't changed.

The woman again just stood there looking now like she was teetering and going to fall over.

"Great." Mikey muttered.

"Okay. Well you have a good Christmas and be on your way. Keep it quiet now. There are all these folks out here trying to get their shopping done. You will scare the kids. Go on now. Move along." Mikey was directing the woman on her way. The woman continued to stay fixed on John.

Before she could snatch her, the woman darted back to John and pulled something out of her pocket. She shoved the item into John's hand and backed away quickly as she saw Mikey swing around now in a much more aggressive stance.

"Freddie. I didn't mean to keep it. I found you with it. It is yours. Merry Christmas, love."

"Lady, I have had about as much of this shit as I am going to deal with on Christmas Eve. Now move your ass along or you can spend the holiday..." Mikey stopped in mid-sentence as the woman turned and quickly hobbled off down the street and into the crowded sidewalks.

"It is getting worse. They are *everywhere*. Now it even seems like they are *importing them*." Mikey was mumbling under her breath as she readjusted her purse and motioned for John to come with her as she escorted him by the arm. They had taken a few steps and Mikey stopped again. She looked closely at John to see his reaction. He seemed to be okay. Wait.

"What the hell did she give you?"

John opened his hand and they looked down at some dirty golden pendant of some sort.

"Yuck. Just pitch that thing." Mikey was gauging the appearance of the woman and then calculating the germ content on its surface.

"Oh, I'd like to keep it. It is my first Christmas present. She *gave* it to me." John winked and chuckled while placing the item in his pants pocket. He started walking again. He wasn't going to challenge her at this moment. Not while her face had that look on it. Best to just keep going. He liked it anyway. It was shiny and truly his first Christmas gift.

Mikey winced and made several gagging sounds. She couldn't wrestle it off of him here in public. Yuck. She managed to mumble several obscenities so that no one could hear.

"Whatever, John. Just wash your hands as soon as we get to the apartment. Disgusting." Mikey was shaking her head and careful not to instinctively reach out to *that* hand while they walked until it had been thoroughly scrubbed. She knew he was purposely ignoring her.

They went to the apartment building with several bags of supplies they picked up along the way. They would cook and watch television for the remainder of the evening. That was the plan. John convinced her that Steve showed him how to cook lasagna. Mikey was sure they would burn the building down. She laughed to herself. Christmas day headline - two idiots burn down apartment complex – film at eleven. Great.

Despite her concerns, the evening went well. They managed to prepare their concoction and not ignite one single spark. The remainder of the evening went by while watching the traditional Christmas lineup. The BB gun story, Rudolph, the Grinch, Frosty, etc... Mikey actually felt a pang for the first time in a long time. She remembered watching those shows so long ago with the family she now was missing very much. She tried hard not to do that. She did seem to find some amusement at John watching these same shows from her childhood memories. She imagined her own reaction to them the very first time. She was sure it was accurately reflected in John. He was delighted. She was happy. After the last scheduled show on their list, she had planned to go home. It had been a hectic several days. She was a little tired.

"Michela? You really aren't going home. Really? You are going to wake up Christmas morning all by yourself. Why don't you just stay? Please. You know Steve won't say anything. He isn't even checking. It just seems like a waste of time. You'll be right back over in the morning. Michela. Please, just stay." He was blocking her path to the door with his arms outstretched.

Mikey started to laugh.

"It looks like you are waiting for a password. You look ridiculous. John, I will be back in the morning. I will. Promise." She smiled and he walked over to her and wrapped his arms around her hugging her tightly. She was saying her goodbyes until the mood switched quite rapidly. What seemed to be a parting gesture quickly solidified her presence for the night. He always seemed to achieve that which he had set his mind upon. Mikey again lost this battle but it wasn't long before she wasn't sorry that she did…

"Merry Christmas." John whispered softly into her ear.

"Merry Christmas." Mikey whispered back just before they fell asleep.

———•—•———

Mikey and John slept late Christmas morning. Mikey was trying to will a coffee pot into existence while she listened to John go over a list of things to do for the day. She laughed when he suggested they make cookies. He was definitely trying to get into the headlines. Surely they would burn the building down this time. Or, maybe even poison themselves trying to eat them. She decided that she could make a quick run to the local convenience store close to the apartment. She would buy some instant coffee since John had no coffee maker. She had been thinking of things to buy *him* for his place but had never considered a self-sustaining gift such as a coffee pot. She laughed to herself. She would also make a list of items they would need for cookies and see if they could pull off the whole cookie caper without having to dial 911.

Mikey dressed quickly and promised she would be back before John exited the shower. She exited the building and the cool, crisp air was some relief. It seemed to have a small impact on waking her senses in the absence of caffeine. She quickly walked to the car, hopped in and sped off to the local convenience store. It would probably be the only store open today. The few items she needed would cost more than a week's worth of groceries. She laughed out loud. Cookies. Where did she lose it? The ability to find joy in some of the simple things life offered? She sat at the light getting lost in the thought. The years watching some of life's most horrifying moments seemed to have become normal for her. It also seemed that in the transformation, the everyday experience was slowly erased to make room. Why did this seem trivial? It wasn't. It should be *fun*. The honking behind her jetted her out of her thoughts and she pressed the pedal hard to forget about what she had been thinking.

Mikey pulled up to the convenience store. It was packed. As she feared, it was probably the only place open today. Everyone else was here too. Great. They were in the same boat as she trying to find last minute items for their days festivities. She quickly scanned the aisles for the items she needed. She managed to find a small jar of instant coffee. Definitely number ONE on the list. She began the list for a simple cookie recipe she found on her Blackberry. Not going so well she thought as she searched for baking soda. She went to the dairy aisle and discovered several prepackaged rolls of cookie dough. Mikey sighed out loud. There was a God and He was definitely looking out for her today. She grabbed the four existing rolls from the cooler and replaced the now unnecessary items. Why did John want to make cookies anyway? Who was going to eat them all? Irrelevant. It was his first Christmas. They would do whatever he wanted. She did love to see him smile when they did something for the first time. She shook her head and proceeded to the check out with her coffee, dough and two aluminum trays. Ah, the simplicity was refreshing. Mikey was getting used to this. She warned herself that in three days, she would be back to work. This was not something that was going to last forever. She had to keep it in perspective and not let it run away with her.

"How much?" Mikey squeaked at the clerk.

"Fifty-three dollars? You are kidding, right?" Mikey shook her head in disbelief. "Highway robbery." That is what it was. She mumbled under her breath as she pulled out the bills. Price gouging. Her face contorted as she grabbed the bag and headed for the car. Mikey slipped into the seat and started the engine. She radio came on and began playing *Jingle Bells*. She caught herself. Holiday spirit. Holiday spirit. Holiday spirit. She chanted to herself as she drove back in hopes of keeping her mind cheerful for this special holiday with John. Holiday spirit...

Mikey and John were up to their elbows in dough most of the morning and early afternoon. Thankfully the dough eliminated the need for bowls and other items that would surely have been scarce. The smell of the cookies filled the air of the apartment. They talked. They baked. They talked. They baked some more. It seemed the dough would never end.

Finally the last batch had emerged from John's oven. There was a mountain of chocolate chip and sugar cookies on the counter. Mikey erupted laughing. She had fought him to not *eat* the cookies as they while they were making them. Now she wished she had let him eat as many as he wanted. It must have been a habit from way back. She remembered the smell in the house and her mother keeping close guard until the bounty was finished. They had been like vultures... Mikey stopped the memories and shook her head. She had never considered she could be like her mother. She laughed out loud.

"John, who is going to eat all of this? Not me! Ha ha ha. You are on your own. I hope you are hungry for leftover lasagna and a whole bunch of cookies. I hope you are prepared for a stomach ache too." Mikey was laughing out loud looking at the ridiculous pile they managed to create from the large tubes of dough. She should have bought less. It would only have been fifty-one dollars! She rolled her eyes while sipping the bitter black serum that had to pass for coffee today. It would do.

John stood and smiled at the mountain and seemed proud at the accomplishment. He seemed to pose like a ninja for a brief moment and then quickly snatched a cookie from the pile. He chomped on the golden disk and began chewing.

Mikey waited for a reaction. She hadn't considered they would taste bad. So she waited for his reaction.

John kept chewing.

"Well?????" Mikey was impatient as there was no discernable reaction.

"Are they good?"

It seemed like he stood there for an eternity. Mikey was getting impatient when he finally looked at her. She was inspecting his face.

"Mmmmmmmm." He smiled and reached for another one.

Mikey started to laugh relieved.

"You had me worried for a minute that we spent fifty bucks on a million crappy cookies!" She snatched one herself and gave it a quick taste. It was warm and good. They weren't quite as good as the ones in her memory that her mother made, but they were pretty good. She nodded in satisfaction.

Mikey reheated the lasagna and they finished it while watching *It's a Wonderful Life*. She remained mostly innocuous to its effects. She had enough of memories for one day. She was glad that John seemed to enjoy it. She was amused while watching him these past few days. He experienced every emotion and every experience portrayed on the electric screen. It was so honest. It was almost hard to observe at times. It made her feel cynical. Maybe she was. They finally reached the movie's conclusion. It was late afternoon. Her phone made a series of beeps. She went to the table and checked her purse for the phone. It was a message from Harris wishing her a merry Christmas. She quickly typed a reply and placed it back in the bag. She had three more days and it was back to work. She was really starting to enjoy the separation from the dark, solitary world she had become such a part of during the last five years.

14

"**M**ichela. Why don't we *give* them away?"

Mikey was watching the Grinch for the second time and was startled by the question.

"What?"

"The cookies. Why don't we give them to someone. How about the police department or the mission?" He was up and thinking.

Great. Mikey knew that something was coming that she wasn't going to be able to stop.

"Yes, like our gift. To someone else. Mikey? Where could we take them?"

He was overwhelmed by the Christmas spirit. This meant a road trip. Great. The PD was out. No one there could know about the *them* aspect of this whole thing. Malfeasance. Yes, she was reminded. The mission was probably overflowing with generous donations for the night. These were the days that people actually showed their true colors and gave. Uh… she was faltering here. The hospital…

"Why don't we go to the hospital and give the wonderful people who helped you a Christmas present? They are there working and without their families?" Mikey waited for his reaction.

"PERFECT! They gave me the gift first and I can return it. Well, maybe…" John trailed off. Mikey could see he was struggling with the comparison of life versus cookies.

"Hey, those nurses would love to get a hold of some freshly baked cookies. They are working the holiday and surely the gesture would make them feel better. And, they sure like you, John. You would be the best gift they could receive. Let's go." Mikey jumped up and grabbed her purse. He seemed a little hesitant, but with a little prodding, was helping to pack all the cookies onto paper plates. They packed the ten plates of cookies into plastic bags and headed out for the car.

The drive to the hospital was quick and quiet. John hardly said two words. Mikey wondered why his mood had changed. She pulled into a reserved police spot close to the door. Habit. They hopped out carrying their bags and went in the emergency entrance.

Mikey led the way to the security desk. After a few minutes talking to the officer, he waved them on into the secure halls of the hospital. It was after hours and necessitated a little professional courtesy. Mikey quickly made her way to the familiar floors that had housed John Doe.

"Would you look who is here!"

Mikey smiled at the white clad women behind the station desk as she and John approached it.

"Merry Christmas, ladies." Mikey quickly remembered Arlena from her first visits. Arlena must have recognized her as well. Although, no one was looking at *her* right now.

"We have brought you a little Christmas cheer." Mikey lifted a bag containing several plates of cookies in it over the counter and placed it upon the desk. The three women were still completely focused on John.

"I just can't believe it. He... excuse me... You look great!" One of the nurses managed to remark.

"Thank you." John seemed to be smiling now and more at ease.

Mikey felt a little uncomfortable at the silence.

"John wanted to bring these over to the hospital. He helped make these. I suppose we could take the rest to the other station. Is that okay?" Mikey figured John may remember those nurses more since he was actually awake while they cared for him. She hadn't considered that he wouldn't remember these first caregivers. It made sense.

"Oh, I'll take him. They will be so delighted." The nurse jumped up and came around the desk taking John by the hand.

"I'm Cindy. I just can't wait until the other girls see you. They won't believe you're here. Come on." The woman continued to chatter as she led John down the hallway.

Mikey reasoned that John was okay and may be more inclined to talk if she weren't with him. She remained a moment to talk to Arlena.

"So? How did you get stuck on the holiday night shift?" Mikey was making conversation to pass the time.

"Oh, you know. The same old thing. Seniority, politics and paying the bills..." The woman rolled her eyes and they both laughed. The conversation went smoothly.

The phone rang and Mikey noticed that Arlena's demeanor changed completely. She turned her chair and spoke in a hushed tone. Out of respect, Mikey turned and walked some distance from the desk to give the nurse her privacy. The call was brief and Mikey returned to the station. It was obvious that the woman's mood had changed.

"Are you okay?"

"Oh, yes. I am." She looked away from Mikey.

"Okay. I'm sorry. I can go now if it is not a good time. I'll go and find John." Mikey nodded at Arlena.

"Oh no. It isn't you. Well, I am not supposed to talk about it, but I guess I can make an exception in your case since you *are* the police." Arlena seemed agitated.

"Well, the hospital got some patients today. The story is truly awful. Everyone is talking about it quietly. It hasn't made the papers yet but I am sure that it will. Those poor people." The woman trailed off.

"What happened?" Mikey was now curious and wanted to listen to pass the time. She was beginning to wonder how much longer John would be and if one of the nurses had possibly abducted him which would be why it was taking so long to pass out cookies.

Arlena looked quickly in either direction and leaned forward so she could lower her voice.

"Well, it all started about three days ago from what I understand. Some worker got scared or maybe had some conscience due to the holidays or something and went to the police. Let me start at the beginning. I guess there was some sort of 'home' for the disabled up north near the Canadian border. This place was some private place that had been around for a long time providing care for people whose families couldn't care for them. I guess it was pretty big and located in some remote area. Well, anyways, over the years it started to lose money. You see, some of the patients families had passed away or just stopped paying and couldn't be found. So the place started to apply for government funds for those patients. They weren't receiving much and over time needed more room for *paying* customers. Oh, I just can't believe it..." The woman put her hand to her face and was trying to regain her composure.

Mikey waited patiently now interested in the story.

"Ok, they began to look through the files of the patients. They found the ones whose families lost contact with the patients and stopped paying or the ones whose families died and the estates didn't have any more money. These patients had no one checking in on them and were a drain on the business. So they decided to get *rid* of them. Not kill them right there or anything. They had a small group of the staff start to take these patients over time to different places so that no one would suspect anything and just dump them off. Just like that." The woman was again becoming visibly shaken and paused replacing her hand to her mouth.

Mikey stood at the desk with the distasteful image becoming fully clear in her head.

"I'm sorry. It is just so awful. So, I guess this one worker went to the authorities and told them what she knew about what had been going on. She hadn't been involved with all of these cases but told them where three of the patients had been dumped off. I guess there were more but she only knew details about these three. The police went and found the three patients. One had died along some highway and the two others were located in some small community hospitals suffering from a number of injuries due to the lack of treatment after they were abandoned. Those are the two we have here now. We were the largest facility with the available bed space. The hospitals in the big cities were full and couldn't accept them. So, they arrived here yesterday. It is so sick. We have all been so sick over it. How could someone just dump a helpless human being off somewhere to just... die. They couldn't take care of themselves. They are severely handicapped. Who knows how long this went on and how many of these people were left out there. It is just so... *sick*. They were supposed to *care* for these poor people. There was no one who would be looking for them." The woman stopped again and began to wipe at her eyes.

Mikey stood there taking in the story. It was quite tragic. And, it explained the absence of many workers on the floor. Mikey shook her head. She began to methodically imagine the investigation of such a case – the interviews with the workers; the search warrants, the examination of all facility records... It would be huge if this had happened over a long period of time. Not to mention, the publicity this kind of story would get. She winced at the thought of the amount of work along with the sense of urgency to locate these people that the investigators must be feeling. The pressure was on for those cops. She felt equally sorry for them as she did the unfortunate souls that Arlena described. The two women stood silently for a while with the mental images that the story left hanging in the air.

"Anyway, I am sorry. I shouldn't have told you. It probably just ruined your night. Oh, maybe even your holiday. I am sorry. It just has been making me sick these past two days." The woman managed a weak smile at Mikey.

"Hey, no problem." Mikey reached out and patted the woman's hand.

"It is part of what we do. I think it does help sometimes to talk about it. I know we've both seen some really terrible things. I know just when I think I have seen it all, something comes around the corner and shocks the crap out of me. Wow. Arlena, that is really sad. I hope they catch every one of them. I'll bet they do. That is a case that I would stay up for weeks working on. I'll bet they find some of them and what is even more important, they will make sure it doesn't happen to anyone else." Mikey had put a partial plastic mask on to reassure the poor woman sitting in front of her. She tried her best not to let her face show the futility of that type of case to the woman. She used the mask to possibly cheer her up and provide some positive feedback.

"You really think they will find any of them?" Arlene looked hopefully.

"I'll bet you fifty bucks." Mikey said confidently and smiled.

"I am glad I told you. I do feel a little better. I hadn't thought of that. It gives me a little hope. Thank you." Arlena's sad face seemed a little relieved.

"You are welcome. And, look who the cat drug in? They finally have had enough of John." Mikey gestured down the hallway.

Mikey watched as John walked the distance between them with four nurses in tow. He was smiling from ear to ear and seemed engrossed in answering questions from four different directions. The cookie mission had been a success. John had managed to give out his first Christmas presents. Well, maybe not the first one. She yawned. It was getting late and Mikey was feeling tired. She also noticed that she had been in these same clothes for two days and really could use a shower. She watched John's face as he approached and he was looking at her smiling. She knew he wouldn't let her go home on Christmas night. She could at least swing by her house to pick up some clothes before they returned to the apartment. She tried to put a smile back onto her face after her visit with Arlena and remove the images from her mind.

Plastic.

"Did you enjoy your visit?" Mikey smiled unequalled by the Cheshire Cat.

"Yes! They are all so nice. I did enjoy the visit." John was beaming.

"Good. Well, cookie man, shall we? We should be going." Mikey thanked the adoring crew and gestured toward the exit. She was pleased. He had a good day. She informed him of the clothes situation and her need to go home. The protests started immediately, but she assured him it was only a pit stop. It seemed to ease the qualm of the situation.

The drive to the house was pleasant with John relating his *first* Christmas and the surprise for the nurses. He was beaming that they loved his gift and Mikey was satisfied that the evening had been a success. She snaked the car along the familiar streets arriving at her house. She left John in the car while she ran inside to gather what she would need for her overnight visit. She surely would be home tomorrow night as the holiday will have passed. She quickly filled her bag from the checklist in her head and went back to the waiting car.

Mikey began driving the familiar path back to John's apartment. She realized that she was really tired. She also noted that John's enthusiasm had seemed to have diminished as well. She figured that he was probably tired too. The last few weeks had been a barrage of activity and emotions. All new to him and some to her as well. He must be exhausted. Mikey decided that she would make sure that tonight would end early so they both could catch their breath. Her vacation was coming to a close. How different it would feel now? She stopped herself from thinking about it. They pulled into the apartment lot.

John spent the remainder of the evening taking in the last of the holiday programming on the television. He didn't want to miss even one. Mikey sat next to him on the sofa tuning in and out of whatever John was watching. Mikey had remembered to grab a small portion of her nightly serum and put it in the overnight bag. She was quietly sipping from the glass. She was beginning to get the familiar warm feeling from it and was anxious to completely relax.

The last show was over and the two retired. Mikey hadn't become completely comfortable before she heard the soft breathing next to her. He was already asleep. She had been right. He *was* tired. She was too. She stared blankly at the darkness. She wasn't completely relaxed as she had expected. Even the small amount of anesthetic hadn't seemed to do the trick tonight. What was it? It was like a small stone in her shoe. This had been at the back of her mind all evening giving her a small sense of annoyance. Mikey began the usual search of her mind and decided to just leave it for tomorrow. She was too tired to unravel her mind at the moment and willed herself to sleep.

Her dreams were vivid but incoherent. They were a series of images and sounds that seemed so unrelated but that kept repeating throughout the night. The final image of a rotting corpse along the roadway yanked her out of the fitted sleep and sent her to a sitting position. It was dark. Mikey realized she had been dreaming and was damp with sweat. She quietly slipped from the bed and tiptoed out of the bedroom and closed the door. She made her way to the kitchen and turned on the light. Mikey realized that she was now wide awake. Going back to sleep was likely impossible. She decided to return to the sofa and sit with another glass of the Black Velvet to slow her racing mind. She hated nightmares, or whatever that was.

She sat stiffly with glass in hand. She allowed her mind to wander and release the tension of the images. She considered that it just may have been the story from the hospital that reemerged in her dream. She allowed the images from her dream to float back into her conscious mind. The colors and haphazard images were less vivid than they had been only a few minutes before. Mikey tried to remember them. She sat there recounting all that she could remember. It was a big ball of mixed images. She sat there allowing her mind to unwind them. Her face grew tight as the images fell into some type of order. These images seemed to blend with memories and they became less random as each second ticked and her brain churned them into a solid mass.

Mikey jumped to her feet with her eyes and mouth wide open. OF COURSE! Her mind screamed inside of her head. She stood frozen in the dimly lit room with her eyes focused wide on the mental image that was now becoming very clear in her head. Why hadn't she thought of it before? She had been so distracted that she did not see the connection of all the little dots that had been forming in front of her. She snapped out of the trace and quickly looked at the clock on the wall. It was three 3:56 a.m. If she left now, she could go home and begin. She had two days. She decided that she could start right now. Mikey discarded the beverage and tiptoed back into the dark bedroom. She heard the soft breathing and realized she still had not awoken John. She went very slowly to the dresser and felt along its top for the objects she remembered seeing there. She tried to be careful not to knock anything off that would make noise or cause her to lose the items she sought in the dark room. There was one. She placed it into her other hand while she returned to the dresser top to find the second item. There. She again crept out of the room and shut the door. Mikey went quickly to the kitchen and found a piece of paper and then a pen from her purse.

John:

Something has come up at work. I had to leave. I probably won't be back here tonight. Sorry. I didn't want to wake you. I'll try to call if I get a break. Get some rest. You seemed really tired. See you tomorrow.

Mikey

Mikey slipped out of the apartment with her purse and bag and almost ran for the car. She raced out of the parking lot and quickly on the route home.

15

Mikey fumbled with her house key. She scrambled inside searching for the light switch. She took a moment to calm herself. She was rushing and would surely forget something if she didn't pull herself together. She inhaled and exhaled a few times. The familiar sense of control started to return as she stood there concentrating. Her eyes opened and she felt more purposeful now than frantic. That was good. Mikey went to the bathroom. First things first. She jumped into the shower. Her mind began ticking off a list in her head of things to do and items that would be needed. She had finished showering and proceeded to her desk to write the list so she would not be distracted from it later.

Mikey went to the computer and turned it on. While it was booting, she grabbed her cell phone and made a call. Thankfully Arlena answered and she was able to get the information she needed. It was in Avondale. Mikey quickly went to driving directions and formed and printed a driving map from Porto San Francesco to Avondale. She frowned. Six hours away. She looked at the clock. It was just after 5:00 a.m. That would put her there at 11:00 a.m. She had better get going. She grabbed the list and packed another overnight bag. She shook her head. She hadn't slept away from home in more than five years and now she was getting to be a pro at it.

The sun was coming up and Mikey was racing north on the freeway. Her head was so full of thought that she hadn't bothered to turn on the radio. There was enough noise in her head already. She decided that she would make a stop around 8:00 a.m. so she could make her next phone call. Two more hours of freeway and double checking her mental list to go.

"Avondale Police. May I help you?"

"Yes, I would like to speak to your Detective Division please."

"Certainly. Please hold."

Mikey waited in her parked car. She had found a rest stop and had purchased coffee and a danish. She would wait until after the call to inhale them and get back on the road. Hopefully she would get the assistance she was looking for.

"Detectives."

"Yes, hello. I am Detective Solitro from the Porto San Francesco Police Department. I would like to speak to the lead detective in the care facility case up there."

There was a silence on the other end.

"Hello?"

"Uh, yes. How do you know about that ma'am?" The voice did not seem receptive.

"Oh, well, I happened upon it while I was at our local hospital. I know it has not been released. I want to offer the detective some assistance here if I can." Mikey was trying to withhold her source out of loyalty and was purposefully vague.

"Hold on a minute." Click.

Mikey tapped her fingers on the wheel and looked at her watch. Every minute extended the trip. She was growing impatient.

"Detective SinClair."

"Hello, Detective. I am Detective Solitro. How are you this morning?" Mikey was attempting pleasantries before diving into the audacity of inviting herself into this man's investigation.

"Yes, Detective. May I help you?" The voice seemed impatient.

Mikey realized that this man was probably the one in the mess she imagined in the hospital.

"Yes, I think you can. I am on my way up there. I would like to offer you a little information that may be connected to your case. I know you must be really busy. I will only need about ten minutes of your time and I'll be on my way. I'd really appreciate it." Mikey felt the need to plead to the man for the small amount of time.

"Well Detective, I have a fairly packed schedule today. When are you going to get in?"

"Sir, I can be there roughly at eleven." Mikey was already starting the car and backing out of the parking space getting a jump start on the long drive ahead.

"I think I can do that. I won't have long. I'm sorry. But I'll make a few minutes for you since you are taking the time to drive all the way up here."

"Thank you Detective SinClair. I'll see you at eleven." Mikey flung the phone on the seat and pressed the pedal further to reach her destination on time.

———•———

Mikey entered the small brick building and went to the information window. She waited for the attendant and noticed it was 11:05 a.m. She was late. She exhaled loudly. A woman popped in front of the window.

"May I help you?"

"Yes, I am here to see Detective SinClair. I am Detective Solitro." Mikey handed the woman her identification and badge.

"I'll let him know you are here." She nodded and smiled at Mikey while picking up a telephone to announce the visitor.

A metal door buzzed and then opened to her right.

"Detective. Hi. I am Don SinClair. I spoke to you earlier." The very distinguished man smiled and held the door open for her to enter.

"Hello. Thank you. I am sorry for being a few minutes late." Mikey quickly entered the open door and followed the man to his office.

"Well, as you may have guessed, we are up to our ears in this one. How exactly are you involved in this one, Detective?"

Mikey noted that the desk was piled with papers and files and the man sat impatiently waiting.

"Well, we had a case uh, roughly six or seven months ago that involved a John Doe. I know you are probably just beginning to identify the possible cases. I just wanted to bring you a picture of the man we found and possibly someone at the facility can match the face to a patient and a possible name."

"Why would you think he may be one of *our* victims?" The man's face was showing some exasperation.

"It is because this John Doe was diagnosed as having a disability. A very debilitating disability. I combed the usual areas and no one had seen him before. It was like he just appeared out of thin air. I would like to leave this picture. It is the only one we have. But, I thought it would be worth a shot." Mikey produced a picture of John Doe. She looked down at the flimsy papered image. They had taken pictures while at the shopping center. There were three altogether. One of John Doe, one of Mikey and one of them together. She withheld two and gave the man the photo of just John Doe.

The man reached out and took the picture and looked at it. He made a quizzical face.

"He doesn't *look* disabled." The man muttered out loud while looking at the photo.

"Yes, I know. There was an accident. The man received medical care and has made a miraculous recovery. He, however, has no memory prior to the incident. So, he hasn't been able to give me any leads as to his identity or origin." Mikey tried to think of a better way of stating the facts, but there was no real way to explain the miracle of John Doe. So, she shrugged and waited.

"Alright, Detective. I have scheduled interviews with the workers. They will be continuing today and all day tomorrow. I should know something by then." The man nodded and took the picture.

"How should I contact you?" The man reached for a pen and paper.

Mikey felt that he had accepted the task. His face had changed and it almost looked kind. She was relieved.

"Here." Mikey reached for the pen and scribbled her name and cell phone number on the paper for the Detective.

"Alright Detective Solitro. I'll see if your John Doe was one of our victims and call you tomorrow. I am sure that soon when this hits the media, I'll be flooded with thousands of John Doe match requests. So, I might as well start with yours." He managed a small smile.

"Thank you. I really appreciate it. I don't want to take up anymore of your time." Mikey quickly stood up and reached out her hand. She shook the man's hand firmly and began to turn to leave. What was she forgetting?

"Wait. Detective SinClair? It may be nothing, but I have some reason to believe that our John Doe was only possessing one object when he was found. I am still not sure if he had it or if maybe someone gave it to him there. But, nonetheless, it was an oval St. Christopher medal. Gold in color. Here." Mikey reached into her pocket and retrieved the object and handed it to the man.

"Just wanted to let you know that. Thanks again." Mikey finished turning her body and went to the door leading back to the lobby.

It was now 11:30 a.m. The six hour drive would put her back in town around 5:30 p.m. She decided that she would pick up the trail that she failed to detect months earlier. She would start at the pier. She tried not to think too much. She actually feared she could become so engrossed that she would drive straight off the highway. Her stomach was in a knot. She wanted to identify John Doe. She was also afraid of losing John Doe once he was christened someone else. She felt very conflicted. She squinted her eyes looking for the safe plastic mask that would get her through this day.

———◆———

Mikey pulled up to the pier. She noticed that some of the fishermen had already left. She hadn't counted on having to stop several times for breaks on the way back. She looked at her watch. It was just after 6:00. Mikey jumped out of the car and walked stiffly to the pier. All the driving had her legs feeling like wooden logs. She tried to stretch them as she walked. She searched up and down looking for a familiar character. Mikey stopped and looked north and south. She sighed. Maybe he had left. No, wait…

Mikey's eyes focused on a figure about 200 yards away. She couldn't see any features, but the telltale body movements were just what she was looking for. She hobbled quickly toward the image. Mikey was getting closer. She was looking and …yes, that was definitely the person she was seeking.

Mikey walked up to the man who didn't seem to even notice her.

"Good evening, sir." Mikey looked at the man who again did not seem to acknowledge her.

Mikey frowned and then realized her error.

"Good evening General, sir." Mikey now fully remembered her evening here months ago.The marching stopped.

"Good evening. Are you from headquarters?" The general stomped up to her.

"Sort of. I talked to you a while back. I don't know if you remember. But, we talked about your missing soldiers. A man and a woman. Right?" Mikey attempted not to lead the man too much but to get him started on the conversation she wanted to have with him.

"Yes! Damned bastards. They are still missing. The enemy is getting smarter every day. They are *everywhere!*" He yelled very loudly.

"Yes, I know. Would you recognize your soldier if you saw him again sir, er uh, General?"Mikey was trying not to make any mistakes. She was getting anxious and beginning to slip a little.

"Recognize him? Hell yes! He was with me, or us, for about a year I think. Messed up real bad. They must have done terrible things to him. Annie had him up and about again before they snatched him a second time. I think he must have been pretty important for them to take him again, don't you?" The General was close to her face now talking more quietly as if the enemy were listening.

"Maybe. I don't know yet. I want to show you a picture. Would you look at it for me?" Mikey had one picture of John Doe left. She winced at the fact that she was in it too, but this was the General. Like he was going to make some crazy connections or even tell anyone. Mikey thought it was worth the small risk. She pushed the picture out in front of her toward him.

"Let me see here… Hey, that *does* look like our soldier. But, it must have been before they captured him. He didn't look like that after." He remained studying the photo.

"General, I need you to be sure. If he just looks like him just say so. But, I am asking you if that *is* your soldier. Can you tell?" Mikey was carefully watching the reaction of the man with the photo.

"Hmph. Can I tell? Yes, I can tell. Aren't you listening. That is our soldier. Fredrick Wentworth. It must have been before they captured him. Like I said. He didn't look very good when we got him!" The man was almost shouting like the louder he spoke the more the detective would understand him.

"Ok, I see. I understand. And, one more thing, General. The woman? Do you know where they took her?" She was hoping if she played along she may get more information.

"No, I wish I did. I've checked the mission where they hide people. But, I don't like being there myself. I don't go in. They may not let me back out. Best to stay a safe distance and watch. But I haven't seen her. I fear they may be keeping her inside there or down in the tunnel under the city."

"Do you mean the subway?" Mikey tried to get some sense of it.

"Yes, I mean the subway or tunnel or whatever you want to call it." The man was getting clearly agitated. He started to stomp his feet now when he spoke.

"Ok. That's it. Thank you General. You have been a big help to me. I hopefully will find your soldiers." Mikey reached out and took the picture from his hand. He turned and started to march back to his post. Mikey raised her eyebrows and turned to go back to the car.

Mikey headed toward the Central District. She was hoping that she wouldn't be too late. She sped off to cover the distance as quickly as possible. Upon arriving, she quickly found a spot and pulled up alongside the curb. Mikey jumped out still feeling the inability to fully operate her legs. She walked clumsily to the front of the building and pulled the door. Yes! It was open. She went inside. She looked around and it was devoid of customers. She did notice some movement behind the counter and then a familiar face was looking at her. Yes, it was the owner.

"Hello, sir. I am not sure if you remember me, but I am Detective Solitro. I was here some time ago asking about a possible missing person." Mikey gave him the big smile across the counter hoping that he would remember.

"Yes, yes. Detective. I do remember. How are you? Would you like something? I was just finishing up but I have a few things still out?" The man gestured at the remaining items in the counter.

"Oh, I couldn't put you out sir. I see you have already begun to close. I was just hoping for some of your time." Mikey looked at the case remembering she hadn't eaten since early this morning. Yea, she was hungry.

Suddenly a voice came from the back

"Who is it Jacob?" A woman appeared from the doorway behind the counter. She looked at Mikey and smiled.

"Em, remember I told you about the detective that came here a while back?" The man gestured to Mikey.

"Oh, the nice police lady. How are you?" She walked to the counter.

"Good ma'am. Thank you. I... I..." Mikey stopped. She rubbed her eyes. She noticed she was not only hungry, she was getting tired too. Not enough sleep and all that driving.

"Oh dear. Can we get you something?" The older woman immediately noticed that the detective looked a little worn for the wear.

Mikey collected herself and began again.

"Thank you, again. I just came here to talk to the gentleman or maybe now the both of you. I am in the middle of sorting out an investigation and I have some questions if that would be okay." Mikey thought that her comment maybe sounded too official and might have scared the pair behind the counter.

"Please excuse me, it has been a long day. Really, I do have some questions. I was hoping you could help me. I am still working on the case that I came here about before. I think that there may be some connection between my missing person and the one you mentioned to me the last time I was here. I just wanted to check. That's all." Mikey was quickly back pedaling so that she didn't frighten them.

"Oh, I see. Well, yes. We would be happy to help in any way we can wouldn't we, Jacob? Why don't you get her something. She looks tired. Come sit with me here and he'll bring you a little something. You can eat while we talk." The kind woman had already taken Mikey's hand and was leading her toward a table. Mikey opened her mouth to object, but the older man was already in motion behind the counter while she was being seated. There seemed no way to refuse, politely anyway. Mikey managed a smile. They were very kind. And observant.

Before she could really make any small talk, the man was at the table with a very appealing sandwich cut into small wedges. Mikey smiled at it.

"Well, go ahead. We don't mind. It is just us in here. You can talk and eat at the same time." The woman was encouraging her.

Mikey hesitantly lifted a section of the sandwich and took a bite.

"Wonderful!" She managed to mumble out with her mouth full and she started to laugh.

The man sat next to the woman and waited for her to chew and then speak. Mikey swallowed and began.

"The last time I was here, you said something about a woman. She worked here or something. What did you say her name was?" Mikey waited for the answer and simultaneously placed another piece of the sandwich in her mouth. There was an opportunity to chew while they answered. It was *delicious*.

"Yes, Annie. She had disappeared after being with us for such a long time. It was so strange. It left us feeling very upset. Has something happened to her?" The man was apprehensive.

"No. Not that I know of. Um. Well let me start from the beginning." Mikey started with her initial investigation of John Doe. She told them how she talked with a number of people and the facts just didn't connect at first. She told them about speaking with them about Annie. She told them about a man at the pier referencing this same woman. She also mentioned that the first responding officer noted a red haired woman at the scene of the accident that had left before she could be identified. And, her own meeting with such a woman on the streets not long ago that had approached the John Doe she was investigating. She called him Freddie. So did the General. Maybe she was *your Annie?*" Mikey pushed more of the sandwich into her mouth.

"Oh yes, the General." Both were nodding their heads speaking in unison.

"He was her friend. Yes. We sent him clothes and food with Annie every day after she left here." The woman added.

"Well, what do you know about her?" Mikey inquired while eying the remaining slice on the plate in front of her.

"Oh, you will have to ask the Missus for that. Annie told her all about her past once. I never wanted to know too much about it." The gentleman seemed uncomfortable with the current topic.

"Oh, I can tell her. Go ahead and finish closing." The woman offered.

"Okay. Good to see you. I hope you find her." He smiled and hurried off to finish his evening chores.

The woman looked at the plate and then at Mikey.

"You eat and I'll tell you the story. See, this one day, Jacob called me and said there was something wrong. I came and the woman was under the weather. I sat with her in the apartment upstairs while she recuperated. She explained a lot of things to me that day. After that, we decided to see if we could help her. Let me see if I can remember it all…" The woman closed her eyes and began to tell Mikey all that she remembered.

"Her name is Anne Bloom. She said she was from London, England. Not that she had to tell you that. Her accent made it very obvious. She said that she came from a nice middle class family there. She had always loved the arts and had always wanted to be an actress. She was enrolled to attend college at Sussex. They had a fairly good arts program there and her parents were supportive of the idea. Well, Annie said that during that summer before she was to go off to college, she decided that she couldn't wait all those years to complete a degree. She had enough money in her account to support her plan. She hopped on a plane and came to America to go to Hollywood. She thought that maybe she could find a way into the business if she were closer to where the action was. She told me that she went to many auditions. Commercials, movies, TV shows and the like. It went on for a while and she couldn't get any work and the money was running out. I guess like many American girls, she found herself broke and in a spot. I guess she called home to speak to her parents, but they didn't want to talk to her. She said she took a few jobs waiting tables and just couldn't make ends meet. She wasn't welcome back at home. So, she took to a life in the streets, if you know what I mean. With the gentlemen. She said she made money at first, but then got involved with the drugs and alcohol. She would spend the money she made on that and then find herself living in the streets until she could get more money. She said that after about nine or ten years, she had resorted to cheap acts just to get more drugs and alcohol. That's when it happened." The lady made a painful face.

"What happened?" Mikey asked, now finished with the sandwich and fully tuned into the story.

"The *scar!* You see one night she goes off with a fellow and things got rough. He cut Annie's face. I guess it must have been pretty horrible. She ended up in the hospital for a while. They stitched her up but it left an ugly scar. She said her days of making money that way were over. She had nowhere to go and began living in the streets. She came here to start over. She didn't want that life anymore. She wanted to give up the drugs and alcohol so that she could make even a little something out of the life she had left. That poor woman. She was so thin. You could just see she had been through a terrible time. She helped Jacob here every day. She was very likable. I was sorry that she just up and disappeared like that. I have been here helping Jacob after that. I think he got very used to her company. He was really quite sad after she had gone." The older woman seemed full of empathy.

"I see." Mikey said numbly. She was digesting all that was said.

"Did you know about Freddie or Fredrick?" Mikey asked her.

"No. Who is that?" That is the man that had fallen on the tracks. The General said he had been staying with them for almost a year." Mikey waited for the answer.

"No, we didn't. But, now that you mention it, it makes sense. She started asking for men's clothes if we had them and was taking more food home than usual. We just assumed it was because she and the General were hungry. But it could have been because there was someone else there. She just never mentioned it." The lady shrugged her shoulders.

"Thank you. Do you have any idea where I might look for her?" Mikey asked the woman hoping to get a starting point.

"Oh no dear. We don't venture into those places. We are old. It isn't safe you know. But, I would guess the mission or the subway. Those are the two known for it. Well you probably already know that." The woman nodded at Mikey.

"Yes. Well that is where I'll start. I will let you know if I turn up with her or not. Thank you. I mean… for everything."

"You are welcome detective. You just be careful out there. I do hope you find out what happened to Annie. Well and your fellow too." The woman smiled.

"Ok, thank you. I'd better get going." Mikey stood up and smiled at the woman and left the business. So, the odd woman on Christmas Eve – that was *Annie*. And, it seemed she knew John. She called him Freddie. She gave him the medal. The one last connection she had to make tonight before she could go home and try to recover from the long day. She had to find Annie. Where did she find him and where did the medal come from. The two remaining questions for the night. Then it would just be a matter of waiting for the call from Detective SinClair. That should do it. She wished herself luck and climbed back into the car and headed for the subway station near the pier.

Mikey parked the car in a no parking zone near the entrance and placed her police placard on her dash. She knew Kyle might be still working and would be quite pleased to give her a ticket if he found her car here unmarked. She rolled her eyes. Still paying for that. She entered the station and began to search the platform for a red-haired woman. She canvassed the area and then the bathrooms and cubby holes in the station. No luck. She decided to wait a while. It was about 10:00 p.m. The last train would be by soon according to the schedule located on the wall. The part that was still legible and not covered with graffiti. Mikey placed herself on the smallest corner of a bench. The germs in here must be exponential she thought and made a face. Great.

The train came and went and no sign of the woman. Mikey was tired. It was almost 11:00 p.m. She stood up and started for the exit. She went up the stairs and started for her car. She stopped and reached into her pocket for her keys. She found them and looked up in time to see a figure across the street. It was dark but she could make out the outline. A small person, possibly female, looking unsteady. Maybe this was her. Mikey decided to take a shot and walk over. She began crossing the street and saw the figure become more clearly defined in the dimly lit walk. A rumpled person staggering around and then she saw it. That crazy red hair confirmed it as she was approaching.

The woman jerked upright and swayed to one side and slowly then to the other.

"Leave me alone. Now you there, just leave me alone." The woman muttered out in the telltale accent Mikey remembered.

"Annie. Hi. I just want to talk to you. That's all. I'm Mikey." Mikey slowed her approach so not to frighten the somewhat disoriented woman who watched her approach.

"How do you know my name?" The woman looked at Mikey with some curiosity.

"We have some friends in common, Annie." Mikey almost had slowed to a crawl as if she were approaching some strange animal. She didn't want this to go badly. She needed to talk to this woman.

"Annie. I have been looking for you. I talked to the General, Mr. and Mrs. Berwitz, and *Freddie*. We've been looking for you." Mikey was hoping that the mention of his name would gain her some credibility.

The woman eyed her suspiciously. Mum, you must be mistaken. I think Freddie is dead. I thought I saw him, but I think I was wrong. He would have remembered me. He would have remembered…" The woman now teetered so far to one side Mikey jutted forward to catch her.

"Oh, Annie. Be careful." Being this close proved to be painful. The smell of cheap alcohol permeated the air. Mikey tried to breathe out of her mouth to avoid the smell.

"Annie. I think you and I need to talk. Can I take you somewhere to get some coffee?" Mikey figured that a little caffeine may help sober her up enough to have some productive results. Couldn't hurt.

"I could go for another round." The woman wavered in Mikey's arms.

"No, that would be enough of that for tonight. I'll be happy to buy you coffee and something to eat. That is it." Mikey was insistent – no more alcohol. That would end the evening almost immediately.

"But, I'll give you twenty dollars that you can do with whatever you please." Mikey figured it wouldn't hurt to offer a little bribe. She was running out of time. She wanted to identify John Doe.

The woman wobbled to and fro for a moment and looked hard at Mikey.

"I saw you before. Was it you with Freddie? Now I remember. Are you the one keepin' him away from me?"

"No, Annie. I'm not. I'm sorry about the other day. I didn't know. You see, John… *Freddie*… doesn't remember anything. Nothing. You know, before the night in the subway. He couldn't tell me anything. He didn't die. He didn't forget you specifically. He just lost his whole memory. I've been trying to help him find it. At least I have been today. So, will you tell me a few things. We don't have to leave here. Just a couple of questions. That's it." Mikey was bargaining with this woman. She may hold the key to the whole story. Mikey wanted to know.

"Okay. I'll tell ya what I can. Ask away." The woman became unsteady again waving her arm for her to continue. Mikey ushered her to the sidewalk so she didn't fall and hurt herself.

"Ok Annie. It's simple really. Where did you find Freddie?" The name was getting easier to say.

"Oh, it was in the tunnel. He was makin' this God awful noise and I went back for him you know. Me and the General. I took care of him. Yes, I did. Every day. He was my life. I would never have taken him out. But, the fits were getting worse. I just wanted them to see him at the … well the safe place and the people was all pushing us here and there. I couldn't hold on. I heard it ya know? I dream about it every night. I heard him scream. Then they came and took him away. I tried to see him at the hospital. But, they wouldn't talk to me. They took one look at me and sent him off. Some thanks. I found Freddie. He was *mine* and they took him away." Annie started to mumble incoherently now and Mikey was worried that she would lose the opportunity to ask the several remaining questions she had.

"Annie? Did you find anything on Freddie with his name on it? Anything? When you found him?"

"No, only the thing in his hand. He was holdin' it so tight. But, I saw it in a dream and knew I was meant to find him. I kept it with me all the time so I had it after they took him away. When I saw him that one day, I wanted to give it back. Maybe it wasn't meant for me. Ya know? I guess he never really *gave* it to me. He didn't talk at all. So, I thought maybe I should give it back. It's only right." Her head began to slump to one side. Mikey had to hurry.

"Okay, stay with me Annie. How did Freddie get onto the tracks?" Mikey held her breath.

"I don't know. They was all pushing and shoving. They pushed us apart while he was having the fit. I tried to hold on then I tried to find him. I think they just didn't even see him. Like they don't see any of us. He was just shoved out of the way and onto the tracks. That's all." The woman fell over and slumped to the cement sidewalk.

Mikey saw the end of the line for the questioning. She leaned down and picked the woman up. She was ready to struggle, but she was so light. She whisked her up so easily that she almost fell. She carried her down the stairs to the station and placed her inside a small hidden cubby area in the tunnel. No one would notice her there till morning. She would be safe. Mikey pulled a hundred dollar bill from her wallet and placed it in the sock of the woman. She would find it in the morning or the next time she bothered to bathe. She left the station to return home.

The quiet drive seemed deafening. Worse, the arrival at home did little to mute the silence that amplified the screaming inside her head. Mikey plopped down on the couch and knew she couldn't completely reconcile the matter until Detective SinClair called tomorrow. However, she already knew the answer somewhere deep down. Nothing else made sense. Mikey bet herself ten dollars that by tomorrow evening, John Doe would have a name. John Doe. Shit. She never did remember to call him. It was very late. Mikey struggled with the urge to call him and tell him everything. She just wanted him to know she had been working so hard. No. She didn't have the confirmation yet. It was premature. He had been through enough. What if she were wrong? It would be cruel to give him some false hope. She was just going to have to hold on for a while longer. She could tell him when she knew for sure. It was best to just go to bed. She quickly went to the cabinet and poured a very large helping of nightly potion. She was going to need it. Though exhausted, Mikey would not sleep without a whole lot of help tonight.

16

Mikey woke and struggled to feel her body. As soon as she moved she felt an aching in her head. Oh yea. She remembered. Too much Black Velvet. Her head was fuzzy and she was very thirsty. Ugh. What time was it? She struggled to see the clock. Noon. Noon! Jeez. Mikey attempted to force herself up from the mattress that seemed to fight back. Her body felt like cement. The mattress was winning for the first few minutes. She finally forced herself upright. A slight spin. Then she had established her bearings. Hangover. Great. Mikey struggled up and went to the kitchen. Coffee pot. She automatically filled the machine and went to the shower.

Mikey tried hard to put last night into perspective. Sadly the haze of the nightly poison was clouding it all up. She resigned herself to the coffee gods and would sit and think once she had some time to get through half the pot. She needed to call John. She missed him. She just had to get it right first.

Mikey almost crawled from the shower to the kitchen. She poured her cup full and sat down. It was like therapy to smell the hot liquid and begin to sip it from the cup. She was startled by the sound of a buzz coming from under the counter.

Cell phone. She tried to maneuver under the counter to get to the source of the sound. Bonk. Great. Her head hit the counter. She waited for it to hurt. Oh, there it was. Damn. She grabbed her head and continued with the search for the device. It beeped. Argh. Voice mail message. She wrestled through the purse and found the phone. She hit the buttons slowly and retrieved her messages.

"Hello. Detective Solitro? This is Detective SinClair. I need to speak to you right away. Please call me." The man gave a number and then slowly repeated it again. He must have ESP to realize she needed a second opportunity to write it down.

Mikey made a note of the number and tried to clear her head before dialing it. Shit. This was it. She punched the numbers in slowly and waited for the sound of the ring. There it was. One, two, three,…

"Hello?"

"Hello. Detective SinClair. It's Detective Solitro. I am sorry I couldn't get to the phone."

"Oh, no problem. You won't believe this. You really won't." The man's voice seemed strained.

"Okay. I'm ready. Shoot."

"To be honest, I almost discarded the whole idea of asking about the medal you gave me. Well, I got through the interviews yesterday and one of the workers claimed that they knew that what they were doing was wrong and had placed Catholic medals with the patients they left behind. Do you *believe* that? She identified the one you gave me as looking exactly like the ones they had."

Mikey was almost sick. Now, not only was her head pounding, but her stomach felt like it was in a vice.

"Then, I showed the picture. You were right. He was a patient there. I guess he was the designated payee of an estate. When the money ran out, they just dumped him off well over a year ago. The worker confessed to leaving him there in Porto San Francesco. Honestly, I thought you were crazy, but you had it." The man seemed to speak so fast that Mikey had some trouble processing the information.

"Detective Solitro? Are you there?"

"Yes. Did they tell you his name?" Mikey's eyes clenched shut. She wanted to hang up, but the plastic face was even possible in this state and she maintained the phone in her hand.

"Thomas Williams. Yes, some of the uninvolved workers identified him. They were sure of it. Seems that the parents placed him here many years ago and since died. Yea, you know that part from the estate thing. Once the estate money ran out, like I said, they just developed a plan and dumped him down there. From the records, it is truly a miracle that he survived without care."

Mikey was not surprised to hear the word miracle connected with John Doe. Or, *Thomas Williams*. She squinted her eyes tightly shut in an attempt to block out any further information.

"Is there remaining family?" Mikey asked blankly.

We don't know yet. It doesn't seem likely. No one had paid the bills in years or had visited him. He was state funded for a few years so I think he was pretty destitute. And, there were no recorded visitors after the death of the parents. So, they considered him a good candidate for their disposal plan. But, we'll work on it."

"Thanks Don. You have just placed a name to one John Doe. It matters even if it is just one. Thank you again."

"No problem. I am glad you came. It is one more solid count we can add against these assholes. Sorry. It just rips at me." The man seemed truly apologetic

"Yea, I know." Mikey thanked him again and hung up. The last 24 hours had proved to be productive. Yet, there was some sense of loss. John Doe had a name. John Doe had a history. He maybe had extended family that didn't even know he existed. She felt a little threatened by it all. Mikey made a fist. She reminded herself that this was why you didn't get involved with cases. It could HURT. She chastised herself and just tried to be calm and have more coffee. She would call him soon. How would she tell him?

Mikey downed about five more cups of coffee before she had the nerve to call. She dialed the number and heard the successive rings. One, two, three, four…

"Hello?"

"John. It's Mikey. Michela. Uh, I'm sorry about the other night. I need to see you."

"You didn't call me. I was really hurt Michela. You just left me."

"I didn't just leave you John. I never left you. Can I come over?"

"I don't know. I am really confused right now. I am *mad* at you Michela."

"I know. I deserve that. But you really need to let me explain." Mikey pleaded.

" I don't know. You were mean to me. I am really mad."

Mikey was growing impatient with the childish banter.

"I know who you are John Doe." She let the words hang in the air like an 800 pound gorilla.

"What? What did you say?" His voice was now very different.

"I know your *real name,* John Doe." Mikey smoothly said with some small plastic quality that made it sound like she was telling him about the weather.

"You are lying." The voice was getting angry.

"John, I'm not lying. I figured out who you are. Do you want to know or not?"

There was a silence on the other end for what seemed an eternity. Mikey had no stones to shatter the wall of silence. She patiently waited.

"When can you be here?" The voice was still angry.

"In ten minutes." She answered.

"Good." Click.

That was that, Mikey thought. No thanks, no excitement. Just a click. Great. She grabbed a few things and took a deep breath. Good thing she had some training in death notifications. It seemed like she would be notifying him of the death of John Doe today. It made her stomach sick, but it was the *truth.* That was her duty. Good or bad. She would have given him the truth. She couldn't believe that she had actually done it. She should be proud. Then she frowned. She should have done it before. Her senses were all screwed up with the addition of all the emotion. It was a big mistake. John Doe was now paying for that mistake. She exhaled hard and rubbed her face. She had broken the rules and was now suffering the consequences for it.

Mikey jumped into her car. She noticed that there was enough gas for a trip to Central and back. Good enough. Maybe she deserved to run out of fuel and have to push the car as a punishment. Who knew? She sped more than usual along the familiar path to the apartment.

Mikey stopped in the lot and hesitated a minute. She wished John Harris was here. She would have had anyone without the emotional connection to get the words out for her. Someone to take over while she could rebuild the plastic mask and make this all sound like a wonderful thing. She felt like driving off and running away. There was a sense of panic in her gut. She didn't know why. Didn't she do what she had promised him those first few nights? She promised her best. And, she had, in some ways with some fortunate breaks, pulled it off. She knew who John Doe was. Why was this a bad thing? She shook her head and got out. Despite every nerve in her body telling her to leave she refused to run away. Running was for cowards. Mikey was not a coward. She wouldn't start being one now.

Mikey trudged the distance to the door of the building. This was not going to be easy. Nothing ever was. She stood for a moment at his apartment door and closed her eyes. She was checking the integrity of the plastic mask. There was no way to tell if it would hold up. She knocked.

Mikey jumped back when the door swung open very hard and banged on the inside wall. Wow. She recomposed herself and entered. He had walked in and sat on the sofa. Mikey shut the door. She walked to the center of the room and stopped. Mikey was a little confused. Why was he so angry?

"You know why I am here. Are you ready?" Mikey was waiting to be sure John was going to be able to handle this. Maybe she should have called Addison and Steve. She hadn't thought of that before. Maybe she had allowed her own sense of urgency to rush forward too fast for him. She gritted her teeth. Too late now.

"Michela, let me start first. You lied to me and I want to know where my things are."

"What?" Mikey shrugged in confusion.

"You lied. You did not go to work. I called there. And, I am missing my gift and pictures. Where are they?" He finally looked at her glaring. He *was* angry.

Mikey was completely confused. Here she was to tell him the answer to the biggest possible question and he was pissed off. She was stumped.

"Uh, well the police have one picture and the medal. The other one got semi-damaged when I was showing it. I think the third picture is still at my house." Again, Mikey shrugged at him.

"You didn't even ask me. You just took them. They were *my* things." He was still glaring.

"John, I *needed* them. They were just a few pictures and a cheap medal. I'll get you another one." Mikey couldn't believe the direction of the conversation.

"What about the lie?" Again, not one movement.

"Well, yea. I didn't want to tell you where I was going until I was sure that I was onto something. I wouldn't want to get your hopes up and then it all be nothing. So, yea. It was what I do. I just wasn't on the clock." Mikey reasoned that she was in some way, working.

"I see. So I am just another one of your cases that needed solved. That's it." He was leaning forward now and seemed to be even more mad than before.

"No. No. Not like that. I mean, well sure you began as my case. And, yes, it still needed solving. And I did that. I promised you I would in the very beginning. I was keeping that promise." Mikey felt like she was on trial.

"I am not that man anymore. I can make my own choices now. I would have liked to have been a part of my own discovery. I deserved that. What I wanted to know, how much I wanted to know and when I wanted to know it." He was standing up now pacing in front of the couch.

Mikey was floored. She thought she was doing him a *favor*. A big one at that. And here she was feeling like some kind of petty thief and liar.

"You never told me you didn't want to know." Mikey glared back now.

"I never thought you would go behind my back and do things that I wouldn't be involved in. I didn't think I had to tell you ahead of time." He looked out the window.

Mikey was now scowling and had no idea what to do now.

"John. I didn't mean to hurt your feelings. I didn't. I'm... sorry." It was the best she had at the moment. She couldn't believe this had turned into an argument.

"Alright. Please start from the beginning then. I want to know exactly what you did and what you found out. All of it." He didn't turn around to face her. He continued looking out the window.

Mikey felt strange, but decided to fulfill the request. Surely the Avondale Police Department would be contacting him anyway. Better he heard it all from her in advance. She felt awkward standing there looking at his back. She considered asking him to sit, but decided to just begin and see what happened.

Mikey began the story with the dream and how the pieces started to come together. She told him that while at the hospital, she had learned of a story that seemed unrelated at first. She hadn't given it a second thought until that night. She told him about the connection of his appearance here with several references to a red-haired woman and the subsequent connection with his initial condition and the story she learned at the hospital. She described each step of her journey in as much detail as she could remember. She ended with the phone call from the detective this morning. She told him that he was Thomas Williams with no known family as of yet. She exhaled and felt a little tired from all the effort to remember it all. No response at all. He was still just looking out the window.

Mikey stood very still. She really didn't know what to do. She wanted to run over and hug him and she also wanted to just turn and run out the door. It was all so very strange.

It seemed like an eternity. John finally turned around and looked at her. Mikey really couldn't identify the look on his face. It was completely blank.

"Where is she?" He asked her flatly.

"Where is who?" Mikey quickly responded anxious to begin some type of conversation.

"Annie."

"Annie? Oh, her. The woman. I have no idea. Homeless. I guess she could be anywhere. The mission, the subway, the streets. Why?" Mikey was perplexed as to why he wanted to know.

"Ok. I'll find her myself." He began to walk past Mikey toward the closet to get a jacket.

"Why?" She repeated the question. Mikey was still confused by his desire to see the ratty woman from the subway.

"I'll tell you again, Michela. This is *my* life. I have questions that you didn't ask. I'll find out the rest for myself." He was putting on the jacket.

"Okay. No problem. I'll drive you where ever you want to go." Mikey was reaching into her pocket to get her keys.

"No. I want to go alone. So, you are going to have to leave now." He opened the door and held it for her.

Mikey was completely put off. She shook her head. She still hadn't moved.

"It is a little rough down there, John. I really think you should let me…"

"Please. I need to do this. Just go." He was still holding the door.

"Okay. Have it your way. Would you call me when you get back and let me know you are okay?" Mikey began walking toward the door.

"I have a lot of thinking to do. I'll call you when I sort things out. I don't know how long that will take."

Mikey walked out of the apartment door and heard it close solidly behind her. She was clueless as to what had just happened. She numbly walked to the car and got in and headed home.

17

Mikey sat at her desk half seeing the computer screen in front of her.

"Geez, Mike. Are you going to find that address or what?" Detective Harris was impatiently standing next to her.

"Oh, yea." Mikey made a few keystrokes and pulled up the necessary screen.

"There it is." She pointed at the monitor to the address it displayed.

"Thanks. You have been back to work for what? Three days? It seems like you are as burned out as when you left. Pull it together Mike. You have been sitting here like a bump on a log since you got back. What's wrong?" The large man walked to the front of the desk so he could see her face.

"Nothing. I'm just out of the routine. That's all." She gave him a small smile and went back to clicking the keyboard.

The door to the unit flung open and a man marched inside.

"Solitro! My office! Now!" He huffed as he walked by her desk and into his small office leaving the door open.

"Wow. You've been back a whole three days and you are in trouble already. Mikey…" Her partner was shaking his head walking away to his desk.

Mikey was expecting this. Surely her personal *investigation* had been discovered. Surely the Avondale PD had called to link their cases with the one here. Mikey winced as she slowly stood up from the chair. The case had been *closed*. She was definitely in trouble. She turned and walked slowly to the waiting office door closing it behind her after she entered.

"Yes?" Mikey didn't want to just come out and admit it, so she would play along.

"So? You are quite the private detective these days aren't you?" The lieutenant was looking at her with hard squinting eyes.

"I guess so." She wasn't going to even try to lie on this one. She knew she had it coming.

"I send your ass on vacation and you end up covering the state digging up all kinds of shit. I just got reamed by the captain. He wanted to know why he wasn't updated on this case while it was in progress. He said he didn't like being out of the loop. I stood there like an idiot while I half pretended to know what he was talking about. When he figured out I didn't have a clue, he blew his stack. You know he called IA. He sent a team to investigate your activity on this case. Mikey, if it even *looks* like there could be impropriety here, you are sunk. You realize that?" He was speaking softly now but the words were like the hiss of a snake.

"Yes." Mikey didn't look up. She was sure she didn't want to see the look on the face that was speaking in that tone.

"He has recommended that a report be forwarded to him as soon as they have interviewed everyone in connection with this. He has a list. It starts with Kyle for Christ sake. Then to the EMT Elliot, the victim, the witnesses, and all those on your supplemental investigation list. They are probably out there now. Is there anything you want to tell me?" He was now leaning forward in an intimidating fashion.

"No." Mikey looked at him and shook her head in the negative.

"You know it will be better for you if you just cough it up. You disobeyed a departmental directive and reopened a closed case. You are already in big trouble. And, like I said, if there is *anything else*, you can kiss your butt goodbye. Do you understand?" He growled it at her.

"Yes."

"You are now officially on paid suspension pending the outcome of the investigation. Leave your gun and badge. I will contact you tomorrow with the results and any sanctions that are going to be filed. You can go." He made a harsh noise in his throat and began going through the case file the captain had presented him.

Mikey slowly placed the items on his desk and walked out. She walked past the Harris' desk without saying a word. He kept looking at her but she didn't feel able to even begin an explanation. She walked out and proceeded to go home.

She arrived at her home somewhat dazed. How had everything gone so wrong? She went inside and went to the bedroom. She slid into the bed and poured a large drink. She would just watch TV until she got tired enough to go to sleep. There was nowhere to go and no one to talk to. She decided to just sit in this spot and wait.

It seemed to Mikey that waiting was all she had been doing. Until today, she had been waiting for John Doe to call her. He had not. She wanted to call him so many times, but respected his decision to call her when he was ready. Now she would be waiting for the outcome of this. Great. Surely they would find John Doe, the nurses, social workers and her secret would be out. She was done. She began to feel a little sick. She wanted to cry or scream but nothing would come out. She had created one big mess that extended from her career through her personal life. Mikey rolled her eyes before closing them tight. She would just have to wait to see how it all washed out.

Mikey was sitting at the counter with her coffee cup in hand. She hadn't slept well. She tried to linger for a while after waking up but felt so jittery that she had to get up. She showered and was now sitting in her usual morning seat. It would definitely be a long day and it was only 11:00 a.m. She refilled the cup. The cell phone began to ring. She thought about not answering it for a second, but decided there was no time like the present and clicked the button.

"Hello."

"Hello. I figured I should call you. They sent a couple of guys over here today. They were asking me a lot of questions about you. Really. I didn't tell him anything. Is everything okay?"

"Yes, John. I told you about what could happen. And, well… it's happening." Mikey answered him flatly but honestly.

"Well, I didn't tell them *anything* about anything, you know?" He mumbled quietly in the phone.

"Thanks. They may just figure it out anyway. Surely Steve will be able to fill in enough details or even the building workers among others. So it's not over. But, thank you. I appreciate your trying to help." Mikey wanted to ask him so many questions but decided against it.

"That wasn't the only reason I called. I wanted to talk to you about some other things. Would it be okay if you came here today?" His tone still sounded nervous.

"Uh, John. That probably isn't a good idea at this exact moment. I don't know if they'll come back there today or not. They may have more questions for you after they talk to other people. I really don't want them to find me there. It would really seal my fate. I know it's not the same, but we can talk on the phone for now. I probably can come by in a few days after they finish." Mikey was thinking about what she would do after this investigation was over. Whatever the outcome, she'd like to keep John in her life. He had really grown to mean so much to her. Maybe they could move away and she could start over somewhere else. She hoped he had finally forgiven her and they could pick up where they left off. Once she was fired, there was no longer any danger or barriers.

"I guess we could talk over the phone now. I told you that I had a lot to think about. I started to remember things while you were telling me about how I got here. I don't remember everything. I do remember some things. It was creepy at first but it seemed like I got better at it the more I tried to remember. I called the doctor and told him about it. He said that the rest might come back or I may just be left with some missing parts. Either way, it is pretty good." His voice was calm but there was still some underlying tension.

"That's great!" Mikey was surprised to hear that her information had actually *helped* in some way. Maybe that is why he had behaved so oddly.

"I can't wait to hear all about what you remember. Maybe we can take a drive to the pier in a couple of days and spend the whole day in your memories?" Mikey was already thinking aloud. She was anxious to hear about them. She was curious what he could recall about his family and time up north.

"Well, Mikey there is still more."

Mikey sat stiffly now. Did he just call her *Mikey?*

"What?" Her voice was unsteady now.

"I did go and see her, you know. Annie. It took me a while to find her, but I did. We talked for a long time. I began to remember the time I spent there with her. It was a long time. I remembered all the things she did for me. They were things that no one had done for me before. She helped me actually learn to move. No one did that in the place I was before. I remember that sometimes when she would bring me food that she wouldn't eat herself. I realize now that she sacrificed a lot for me. She is really different from what you see on the outside…" He paused.

"Yes, okay. I am sure she is very nice. That is so great what she did for you, John. Maybe we can do something nice for her in return." Mikey was thinking about Dorthea. She would be the perfect person to plan a great gift.

"Well, you see, I *am* planning on doing something nice for her. I will be starting my new job next week. I checked with Steve and we had a long talk. He has okay'd it. I am going to ask Annie to move in with me." There was seconds of silence.

"*What?*" Mikey's voice was filled with disbelief.

"What are you doing John? You can't keep her like a pet or anything. I mean, and what does it look like having some woman living in your apartment?" Mikey was now talking much louder and more quickly.

"It will look like exactly what it is. Two people living life together." He seemed so matter-of-fact about it.

"John. Don't be ridiculous, I mean… You don't owe her that. I thought *we* were together. That we would *be* together. I can't see what you are trying to do here. I mean, look at her, will you? Wait a minute. Are you? Do you mean that you don't want to… see me anymore?" Mikey's voice was unsteady due to the lump forming in her throat.

"It would be the best thing I think. Yes."

"John, why are you doing this?" Her voice was now almost a sob.

"Mikey, please understand. I cared very much for you. I appreciate all the really great stuff you did for me. I will never forget any of it. I know some of it was your job and some of it was not. But, after a short time, I realized who had actually sacrificed for me and truly loved me. It was Annie. Sure, I could walk away and probably be really happy with you. No, not probably. I am sure of it. But, how could I turn my back on *her*? Now, she really needs *me!* The guy at the deli told me how she was before the accident. She was happy and she did really well. That was while she was taking care of me. Then she went back to the old life. Yea, she isn't doing so good right now. That's where I can help. I want to help her back up – like she did for me. She gave me my second chance. I want to give Annie hers. I know I can bring Annie back. At least, I'll spend the rest of my life trying." John's voice was firm and determined.

Mikey realized that not only was she about to lose her job, she had lost John Doe as well. It was overwhelming. She was choking on the tightness in her throat. Was this some kind of sick joke? In less than a week he had decided his whole life. It seemed impossible. Mikey couldn't understand how he could choose this woman over her. She was torn between sadness and anger.

"John, don't do this. Please. It is so soon. You may later change your mind and then what? Are you completely sure this is what you want? You may not be able to go back you know." She was fighting for her chance and maybe she could reason with him.

"Yea, Mikey. I'm sure. From all that I remember, no one in my life seemed to care much about me. They had left me to other people whose job it was to take care of me. For once, there was someone who did it because she *wanted* to. I know I could have a better life with you. Better like having a nice house and things. Going places. That kind of stuff. But, what I can have with Annie isn't like that. It doesn't come from money. It is more a two-way thing. I needed her and she needs me now. I think we belong together. Look, this wasn't easy for me. I really had to fight myself about this one. Believe me, Mikey. I wanted to come back. But, I know this is the right thing to do probably because it is the hard thing to do. Annie and I, we are alike in many ways. Mikey, I chose Annie."

They sat in silence on the phone for several minutes. Mikey couldn't think of anything left to say that could change his mind. He didn't really leave any room for negotiation. He had made his choice. That was it.

"Okay. I understand. I guess that is it. Take care of yourself, John Doe." Mikey managed to squeak out the words.

"I will. You be careful Mikey. I know you'll be fine. You are tough like that. I know this is going to be hard but soon you may even be glad things turned out this way. I won't forget you."

Mikey heard a familiar voice in the background calling the name Freddie. She gulped. She was there with him.

"Goodbye." The voice sounded very final as he spoke the single word.

"Goodbye, John." Mikey pressed the red button and ended the call.

18

$\mathcal{M}$ ikey opened the car door and began to reach into the back to get her things.

"I can't believe you're really going. Are you sure about all of this?" Dorthea was wiping her eyes again.

"Yea, Dot. I'm sure." Mikey continued to pile the bags onto the curb.

"But, don't you think it might be too soon? I'm just saying that so much has happened. Maybe you should just let the dust settle a little more before you just uproot yourself like this." Dorthea seemed to be pleading more than reasoning with her.

"Why? What is there left for me here? Although the PD didn't just fire me after the investigation, the end result was almost the same. They offered to allow me to *resign*. Nice of them. I liquidated the pension I had built up. I sold the house. So, no job, no home, no family, no… well him. I need a fresh start Dot. I can't stay here anymore. Aside from you, I have nothing to keep me here. And, if I know you, you'll find a way to visit me." Mikey was sure that there was nothing left to keep her here. Not even her friendship with Dorthea. Dot had her own life to live.

"I know, but it is so *far*. I mean, could you have found any place further away?"

"Ha. Nope. Guess not. Hey, the job offer came along and I just took it. That's all. It is as good a place as any." Mikey had finally finished unloading the bags.

"You really are moving to Michigan, aren't you? It is so cold there in the winter. You are going to hate it. Do you even own a parka?" Dot was frowning looking at the bags.

Mikey laughed out loud.

"No, but I'll get one if I need it. Hey, I have had enough of all of this Dot. I think this teaching job will be good for me. It will let me sort out who I've become and maybe get back some of who I used to be. You said it yourself. I had managed to make a corpse my friend." Mikey struggled with the raw memory.

"I look back at it and wonder why myself. Maybe it was just easy. In the beginning, John wasn't *anybody*. He was an empty box. I think it was easy for me to project all my thoughts, hopes and dreams onto him. He couldn't object or let me down. It was safe. So, I'd like to figure it all out. Maybe one day I can actually find something like that again but with someone who is real and who *wants* to be with me."

"I know you will Mikey." Dorthea lunged forward and hugged her good friend.

"Do you want me to wait with you until they call your flight?" Dorthea wasn't anxious to leave her friend.

"No. I'll be fine. I'll just grab something to eat and maybe find something to read. It is going to be a long flight. Plus, it will just give you more time to talk me out of this." Mikey winked.

"You suck Mikey." Dorthea gave out a little giggle. She had not hidden her motive very well.

"You do too. I'll call you as soon as I get there, okay?" Mikey smiled.

"Okay. Have a good trip or life or whatever." Dorthea squeezed Mikey one last time.

"I will." Mikey grabbed the boarding pass from her pocket and pushed the cart containing her remaining belongings and went into the airport. She was a little afraid for a moment. This was a very big step. She turned and looked back at the glass doors and took one last look at the place outside she had called home for so many years. There was nothing left for her here. Just memories that never seemed to work out right. She turned and pushed the cart. Maybe it would be different now. She could at least hope.

19

"Annie!" Their voices rang out in unison.

"Hello. It is just so good to be back here." Annie stood in front of the counter smiling at the older couple.

"I can't believe that you are having me back. After I left ya so poorly. I really appreciate this."

"Don't be silly. We are thrilled to have you back at the deli. Now Jacob will let me go back home. How is Freddie? Or, is it… Tom?" Mrs. Berwitz was getting confused with the name changes that surrounded him.

"Oh, Well, I still call him Freddie. It's his nickname now. He said he likes it better than Thomas. He is good. He has been working and we are trying to save up for our own apartment. So, this job is really gonna help out. Really, I do appreciate it. I won't let ya down again."

"Enough of that. Oh, what a lovely necklace. Where did you get it?" Mrs. Berwitz leaned closer and admired the shiny gold pendant half hidden behind the wavy long red hair.

"Oh, Freddie. He gave it to me. It was returned to him after they finished the case up north. He bought a chain for it and gave it to me as a present. He called it a second-hand, second chance gift." Annie lowered her head blushing a little at the personal nature of the item.

"It is lovely. Are you ready to get started on your first official day of work here now that we are actually paying you?" Mr. Berwitz chuckled watching the two women.

"Yes, sir. I am. I think I am ready for about anything." Annie smiled and followed the man behind the counter.